I0640057

William Paley

Letters to William Paley, M.A., Archdeacon of Carlisle

William Paley

Letters to William Paley, M.A., Archdeacon of Carlisle

ISBN/EAN: 9783337272067

Printed in Europe, USA, Canada, Australia, Japan

Cover: Foto ©Andreas Hilbeck / pixelio.de

More available books at **www.hansebooks.com**

LETTERS

TO

WILLIAM PALEY, M.A.

ARCHDEACON OF CARLISLE,

ON HIS

OBJECTIONS TO A REFORM

IN THE

REPRESENTATION OF THE COMMONS,

AND ON HIS APOLOGY FOR THE

INFLUENCE OF THE CROWN IN PARLIAMENT;

BEING

STRICTURES ON THE ESSAY UPON THE BRITISH
CONSTITUTION INTRODUCED IN HIS PRINCIPLES
OF MORAL AND POLITICAL PHILOSOPHY:

WITH

AN APPENDIX.

" Nullæ sunt occultiores insidiæ, quam eæ, quæ latent in SIMULA-
" TIONE OFFICII, aut in aliquo necessitudinis nomine: nam
" eum, qui palam est adversarius facile cavendo vitare possis, hoc
" vero occultum, *intestinum ac domesticum malum,* non modo non
" existit, verum-etiam opprimit, antequam perspicere atque ex-
" plorare potueris."

CICERO *in Verrem.*

LONDON:
PRINTED FOR J. JOHNSON, IN ST. PAUL's CHURCH-YARD.

1796.

PREFATORY ADVERTISEMENT.

THE conjuncture of the times induced me to revize and to amplify fome curfory ftrictures on the feventh Chapter of the fixth Book of THE PRINCIPLES OF MORAL AND POLITICAL PHILOSOPHY; which, when this work fell in my way fome years ago, I fent to a periodical mifcellany.—However frequent the practice, a moment's reflection would teach, that it cannot be the intereft of any one engaged in a controverfy to depreciate the powers of his adverfary; for where is the utility of a conteft with debility? or what can be the credit of a victory? Yet in the prefent inftance I cannot forbear to obferve, that if I were required to defcribe the impreffion this Gentleman's political labours left on the mind of others from their effect on my own, certainly I fhould apply the diftich of the Poet—

" This is mere moral babble, and direct
" Againft the canon laws of our foundation ;"——

and drop all further remark. Of courfe, for a long time I thought a formal anfwer to this production would be needlefs. But after having heard Mr. PALEY's name and work quoted in Weftminfter Hall and in Parliament, as of high authority— now that, I underftand, it is appointed a ftanding book for examination in one of our Univerfities—and when I fee the TENTH edition advertized, befide a feparate publication of this obnoxious Chapter, I muft take his performance to be worthy an inveftigation fomewhat more detailed.

The

The general caſt of theſe elementary diſquiſitions on political topics furniſhes matter for ſpeculation.   After the example of the writers employed by the STUARTS, he has recourſe to the patriarchal ſcheme for the origin of civil Government. We find the original Compact, maintained by LOCKE to exiſt between the King and the People, denied and controverted. There is a defence of the rotten Boroughs.   He extenuates, in fact juſtifies, the Influence of the Crown on Parliament ; and the volume cloſes with an enumeration of the advantages of a ſtanding Army of mercenaries ! I will not however accuſe Mr. PALEY of any oblique motives in having blended with diſ-courſes on the ſocial duties of Man, excuſes for a ſyſtem of diſguiſed venality.   But no one can abſolve him from the re-proach of countenancing practices which, ſo far from having foundation or warrant in the popular genius of our Govern-ment, cannot be carried on but in direct defiance of the Law of the land relative to the mode of conſtituting that Parliament, for which, during their Seſſion, the Archdeacon of CARLISLE is enjoined to put up his prayer to Heaven " to direct and " proſper all their conſultations—that Peace and Happineſs, " Truth and Juſtice, Religion and Piety, may be eſtabliſhed " among us."—

If any where in the enſuing ſheets, I have expreſſed myſelf warmly, let it be remembered that I am repelling an attack on received opinions of conſtitutional Rights—an attack on Rights which I truſt Engliſhmen will never ceaſe to uphold.

In concluſion—ſhould I at all aſſiſt to give a proper direction to the ſpirit of general diſcontent, which poſſeſſes ſome minds, or to diſpel the illuſion of panic-alarm at a Parliamentary Re-form, which clouds the judgment of many, many more, this amuſe-ment of the leizure of the ſummer-months will not have been vain.

November 6.

LETTERS

TO

WILLIAM PALEY, M. A.

ARCHDEACON OF CARLISLE.

───────────

LETTER I.

" Però è bifogno, a voler pigliare autorità in una Republica,
" e mettervi trifta forma, trovare la materia difordinata dal tem-
" po, e che a poco a poco, e di generazione in generazione, fi fia
" condotta al difordine ; la quale vi fi conduce di neceffità, quan-
" do la non fia (come di fopra fi difcorfe) fpeffo rinfrefcata di
" buoni efempj, o con nuove leggi ritirata verfo i principj
" fuoi."
MACCHIAVELLI, Difc. fopra Livio, Lib. 3. Cap. 3.

" He who would alter a Government, and fet up himfelf,
" muft attend till time hath corrupted the mafs, and, by de-
" grees, brought all into diforder ; which of neceffity muft
" follow, when it is not (as we faid before) purged and refined
" by the examples of good men or good laws, *that may reduce*
" *it toward its firft principles.*"
Tranf. 1720. fol. p. 393.

SIR,

ESSAYS on " *Moral Philofophy*" come in a very
queftionable fhape, when fubfervient to a defence
of the depravities of our Conftitution. Look back,
and you will find thofe to have been the brighteft
ornaments of the Church of England who tampered
the leaft with politics. Heretofore the friends of
B. Liberty

Liberty had to contend with formidable enemies, in-
trenched in the ftrong holds of fuperftition, and
many brave men fell before the pulpit-batteries of
divine right and *paffive obedience* were filenced. At
this day, we fmile to fee the fworn foes to the
Rights of Mankind, when driven from thofe intrench-
ments, reduced to fculk behind the flimzey *mantelets*
of Morality to difcharge their feeble artillery.

We have all heard innumerable encomiums on
the excellency of the Englifh Conftitution of State.
Yours, however, Mr. PALEY, far, very far, fur-
paffes every other. It is an hyperbole of panegyric.
The whole fcope of your reafoning is to convince
us that our form of Government is contrived fo ad-
mirably, that incroachments and perverfions, combined with "*flagrant incongruities,*" greatly contribute to its practical advantages! So the value of
an antique ftatue advances in the eyes of fome fantaftic virtuofi in proportion to the mutilations it has
fuffered from the hand of violence, or the injuries of
time.

As your preparatory fketch of what (with no flight
violence to language) you call the "*popular Reprefentation,*" though by no means overcharged, is to-
lerably faithful, it is unneceffary to adjuft the grounds
of our controverfy. According to you, "the
"Houfe of Commons confifts of five hundred and
"forty [fifty] eight Members, of whom *two hundred*
"are elected by *feven thoufand* Conftituents! fo that
"a majority of thefe feven thoufand, without any
"reafonable title to fuperior weight and influence
"in

" in the State, may, under certain circumftances
" decide a queftion *againft the opinion of as many mil-*
" *lions.* Or, to place the fame object in another
" point of view—if my eftate be fituated in one
" county of the kingdom, I poffefs the ten thou-
" fandth part of a fingle Reprefentative ; if in an-
" other the thoufandth ; if in a particular diftrict,
" I may be one in twenty who choofe two Repre-
" fentatives ; if in a ftill more favoured fpot, I
" may enjoy the right of appointing two myfelf;
" if I have been born, or dwell, or have ferved an
" apprenticefhip in one town, I am reprefented in
" the National Affembly by two Deputies, in the
" choice of whom I exercife an actual and fenfible
" fhare of power : if accident has thrown my birth,
" or habitation, or fervice, into another town, I
" have no Reprefentative at all, *nor any more power*
" *or concern in the Election of thofe who make the laws*
" *by which I am governed, than if I was a fubject of*
" *the Grand Seignior*—and this partiality fubfifts with -
" out any pretence whatever of merit or public pro-
" priety to juftify the preference of one place to
" another. Or, thirdly, to defcribe the ftate of na-
" tional Reprefentation as it exifts in reality : it may
" be affirmed, I believe with truth, that about one
" half of the Houfe of Commons obtain their Seats
" in that affembly by the Election of the People,
" *the other half by purchafe, or the nomination of fingle*
" *proprietors of great eftates.*"—*P.* 485. 4*to.* 1*ft edit.*

Ah ! Tantamne rem tam negligenter agere—To bur-
lefque Reprefentation, as well by withholding the

tranf-

tranfcendent franchize of Election from numbers,
whofe qualifications give them a claim that cannot
be refifted *by argument*, as by beftowing it on others,
who, to ufe the fofteft terms, can have no pretenfion
to exclufive preference. After your ftatement, contradictory to all thofe ideas of an Houfe of Commons which we have received from writers the moft
accredited, many will feel it difficult to fufpend their
judgment againft its competency. Inftead of con-
ciliating us to this contracted meafure of anomalous
Reprefentation, perhaps your account of its actual
conftruction will be thought to fuperfede all neceffity
of argument in favour of fpreading an uniform and
comprehenfive right of Suffrage over the mafs of
the People. Waving all other confiderations, it cannot but rufh forcefully into the minds of moft, that
fince Public Opinion ultimately upholds all Governments, to remove this palpable opprobrium ought
to be the firft care with every one rationally attached
to the Englifh Conftitution. I fay the firft care, becaufe it is eafy to forefee that the odium of *fuch* defects in one will unjuftly be transferred to all its
branches. But, whatever may be the conceptions
of others it is now my province to difcufs the queftion with you. It is a queftion in which all have
a common concern; for it is this—Has our Legiflature acted rightly in rejecting the reiterated applications to rectify this medley of arbitrary ine-
quality?

You fum up the grofs amount of the corruptions
in our Reprefentation by affirming, that " *about* ONE

HALF

" HALF *of the House of Commons obtain their seats by*
" PURCHASE, *or the* NOMINATION *of single pro-*
" *prietors of great estates.*" Ought not this por-
tentous truth to arouze every Englishman? If
choice and " *purchase*" be not the fame, then
they who buy their admission into the grand Reprefentative Council of the Nation, can wear no colour
of refemblance to thofe who heretofore received an
allowance from their Conftituents for their attendance. And that " *nomination*" can never compen-
fate the lofs of free election, appears to my mind as
intuitively clear as that neither Reprefentation nor
its benefits can fubfift when a legiflative body is not
derived from popular appointment. Figure to yourfelf my furprife at your unqualified affertion, that
" *the effect of all reasoning on the subject is to diminish*
" *the first impression!*"

Where chicanery is not on the watch to elude,
nor venality at work to canker, time alone will give
birth to many deviations in the beft formed inftitutions. The Land-tax, though adjufted toward the
clofe of the laft century by a new affeffment, has
been for years grofsly difproportionate; fo as in
many parts oppreffively to bear on the land-owner;
in others it is no more than nominal. What wonder, then, that the Commons' Houfe of Parliament,
a fortuitous affembly of which, in the darknefs of
its antiquity, the origin is not to be traced with
certainty, fhould be fallen into diforder, and the
elective powers require to be diftributed afrefh?
The wifeft fyftems, from the mutations of things,

in a tract of years, muft be brought back to their
fundamental principles, elfe they will mar the very
purpofes they were appointed to maintain. " The
" fhadow ferves the fubftance to invade." An adequate and free Reprefentation of the People, fuited
to the exifting ftate of fociety, is the life-fpring
and mafter-principle of freedom in our Conftitution, [App. A.] and was moft affuredly the foundation of parliamentary meetings. But the forms
of conftituting our Reprefentors have receded from
the primary defign fo far that they have become abfurd, and threaten to be deftructive. What happens
to all other human eftablifhments, when the fame
courfe runs on for centuries, has happened to the
Houfe of Commons. In fome Boroughs the Members exceed the number of Electors. Such are the
Boroughs belonging to "*fingle proprietors.*" Is not
this annihilation of the leading idea of Reprefentation glaringly *abfurd?* And when the emiffary of a *Tartar Mahometan* Prince has purchafed
not lefs than EIGHT SEATS among the Commons of
Great BRITAIN in Parliament affembled, which was
the cafe after the diffolution in 1780, it is an alarming abufe that may too juftly be called *deftructive* *.

In a divifion on the queftion, whether we fhould
enjoy the bleffings of Peace, or perfevere in a dif-
aftrous and civil War, the NABOB OF ARCOT has
borne equal weight with the county of MIDDLESEX,

---

* Among others Mr. PITT and Mr. BURKE authenticate
this aftonifhing fact. See App. B.

and the cities of LONDON and WESTMINSTER !—
Are there terms of fufficient ftrength to delineate
this dreadful enormity in fit colours ? What but a
reformed plan of Elections can fhield us from a re-
petition of thefe attacks, which ftrike at our exiftence as an independent State ? The fame inlet
through which the rupees of MAHOMED ALI KHAN
infinuated his agents into *Saint Stephen's Chapel,* you
muft confefs to remain open; and, if your arguments be valid, ought not to be fhut againft intru-
ders from any European power.

But you caution us to " be affured before we ad-
" venture upon a reformation, that the magnitude
" of the evil juftifies the *danger* of the experiment."
The happy fuccefs in the fixteenth century of the
Reformation in Religion, and of the Revolution in
Monarchy in the laft, events incomparably more re-
plete with feeming " *danger*" than any abolition of
the depopulated and venal Boroughs, demonftrate
that any alterations either in Church or State, which
the majority of the Nation approves, are not really
dangerous. Or were they to appearance involved
in " *danger*," Englifhmen, I truft, would exclaim
with the fpirit of the gallant Roman, better an
hazardous freedom than the dead repofe of fervi-
tude *.

To fpeak from " *experiment*," the right of voting
in CRICKLADE and in SHOREHAM has been amended in the prefent reign, by fummoning the Free-

---

* " Potior vifa eft *periculofa Libertas,* quieto fervitio."

holders

holders of the circumjacent Hundreds to their poll-
booths. Not a whisper of complaint has been
heard against this procedure; and it would perplex
the most acute speculator to make out that the
slightest appearance of " *danger*" could possibly arise
from any well-weighed method of diluting a poison in
the body-politic—A virulent poison, which already
deeply corrodes its vitals, and if not soon corrected,
will inevitably destroy the whole.

Yours is the blindness, not the fidelity of friend-
ship. In truth the " *danger*" lies on the other side.
There *is* " *danger*," great and, it may be, imminent
" *danger*" in the rulers of a Nation hearing the call
for Reforms with averted ears. That stubborn sel-
fishness which relies on the strong arm of power to
bear out its hateful usurpations, may indeed endan-
ger the peace and happiness of a country. If salu-
tary truths be scorned on the one side, extravagant
projects will be indulged on the other. Instances
are not wanting to show to you, that planting despair
or disgust in the hearts of those who seek to ward off
a national convulsion by seasonable and temperate
Reformation, impels inconsiderate and ardent tem-
pers to follow their object at whatever risque : while
milder dispositions, desponding, or shrinking from
the threatened shock, leave indignant enthusiasts to
urge on the general dissatisfaction, which conduct so
insensate never fails to provoke. But the affections
of the human mind must be inverted before conces-
sion irritate, or before a redress of public grievances
excite public discontent. I pursue " the wisdom of
" a timely

" a timely Reform" no further in my own words, and now lay before you a canonical text, which I wiſh to ſee blazoned in golden letters on the walls of both Houſes of Parliament.—" Early Reformations are " amicable arrangements with a friend in power : late " Reformations are terms impoſed upon a conquered " enemy ; early Reformations are made in cool " blood ; late Reformations are made under a ſtate " of inflammation. In that ſtate of things the Peo- " ple behold in Government nothing that is re- " ſpectable. They ſee the abuſe, and they will ſee " nothing elſe.—They fall into the temper of a " furious populace provoked at *the diſorder of a houſe* " *of ill fame* ; they never attempt to correct or regu- " late ; they go to work by the ſhorteſt way—they " abate the nuiſance, *they pull down the houſe* *."— So much for your caution on " *the danger of the ex-* " *periment.*"

I am now to obviate an argument of ſome plau- ſibility. You conſider Repreſentation " ſo far only " as a right as it contributes to the eſtabliſhment of " good Laws, or ſecures their juſt adminiſtration. " Theſe effects (ſay you, and truly) depend upon " the *diſpoſition* and abilities of the national coun- " ſellors. Wherefore, *if* men (you add) the moſt " likely by their qualifications to know and to pro- " mote the public intereſt be actually returned to " Parliament, *it ſignifies little who return them. If* * the propereſt perſons be elected, *what matters it*

* Burke ; Speech on his Reform-Bill. Works, v. 2. p. 189.

" *by*

" *by whom they are elected?* At leaft no prudent
" ftatefman would fubvert *long eftablifhed or even fet-*
" *tled rules* of Reprefentation, without a profpect of
" procuring wifer or better Reprefentatives."—P.
487. *Much virtue in Touchftone's* IF, Mr. PALEY.
Permit me to avail myfelf, *è converfo,* of this ufeful
particle. *If* men the moft *unlikely,* by their want of
" *qualifications to know and to promote the public in-*
" *tereft, be actually returned to Parliament,"* which
unqueftionably *has* happened in former, and therefore *may* in future Parliaments, it fignifies much that
the mode be altered—*If* many the moft improper
have ever been elected, through the blind and pre-
pofterous allotment of the powers of Election—
If ever " *the rotten part of our Conftitution, the*
" *fmall Boroughs,* (the ftrong language of BUR-
" NET) have been wrought on to choofe bad men."
[*App.* C.]—*If* the needy and the worthlefs, raw
lads, and fpendthrifts*, gamblers and ufurers, have
not feldom difparaged the Houfe—*If* the Stewards,
or Sons, or younger Brothers of Peers, Officers,
naval and military, practifing Lawyers and Penfioners, Commiffaries and Loan-jobbers, have frequently
gotten Seats, is it not a matter of the moft mo-
mentous urgency that the modes of exercifing the
elective franchize fhould undergo a revifion? Are
fuch " *men the moft likely"* to fuftain the dignified
character, and to fulfil the duties of elected Legiflators? In no other department of the State are

---

* " And if a Borough choofe him, not undone."—*Pope.*

perfons

perſons employed in poſts for which they are ſo obviouſly unfit. See, Sir, to eſtimate the value of the preſent ſyſtem of Election by your own ſtandard, the characters of many " *actually returned to* " *Parliament*," eſtabliſhes that there muſt be an inherent vice in the ſtructure of that body !

Set it in the ſtrongeſt light. Let it be even conceded for the moment, that the identical men would be " *returned to Parliament*" by gratuitous and free Elections, who now ſteal in thither by " *purchaſe or* " *nomination*." A teacher of Morals ought to have known how much the human character is affected by circumſtances. Till you had gravely ſtated, that " *if the propereſt perſons be elected, by whom*" is of little importance, the queſtion would not have borne a doubt, whether the " *dispoſition*" of the ſame man deriving his political exiſtence from public favour to bear the faculties of this great office profitably to the People—is to be aſſimilated to his " *dispoſition*" when he ſeats himſelf by a draft on his banker. How ! Is the ſenſe of obligation nothing ? Are the popular habitudes and talents which recommend a Candidate in popular Elections, nothing ? * Is it nothing to reciprocate good offices ? Is it nothing

---

* " A ſtrenuous reſiſtance to every appearance of lawleſs " power ; a ſpirit of independence carried to ſome degree of " enthuſiaſm ; an inquiſitive character to diſcover, and a bold " one to diſplay, every corruption and every error of Govern- " ment ; theſe are the qualities which recommend a man to a " Seat in the Houſe of Commons in open and merely popular " Elections."—BURKE ; *Thoughts on the preſent Diſcontents*.

that

that we can continue him in the ſtation as long as we approve, and can caſt him off when we approve no longer? You overlook that elevation by Suffrage not only increaſes the probability of perſonal excellence, but induces an aptitude to miniſter to the wants, and a wiſh to accommodate the expectations of the People. Hence the certain " *proſpect* " *of procuring wiſer and better Repreſentatives*" by a well-proportioned ſcale of Election.

Fallacy lives on generalities; and you deal largely in them. I ſhall particularize my obſervations on practices ſo diſtant as our rights of voting from the dictates of common ſenſe. If indeed no adventitious qualities be impreſſed on the minds of the Legiſlators for the Commons, by the deſcription of thoſe who veſt in them that truſt, it " *matters not by whom* " *they are elected.*" But you cannot ſuppoſe the " *Deputies*" certified by a dozen or two of workmen in the dock-yard at QUEENBOROUGH, or by the nominal proprietors of drowned land at St. MAWES, to be votaries to the public good, are as likely " to " protect in the Legiſlature the rights of the Re" public of Letters," as the Members for our Univerſities. In another place, " *the variety of tenures* " *and qualifications, upon which the right of voting is* " *founded, appears to you a recommendation of the mode* " *which now ſubſiſts, as it tends to introduce into Par* " *liament a correſponding mixture of characters and* " *profeſſions,*" *p.* 489. So then you cannot be quite clear that the provincial Repreſentatives have the ſame feelings for Commerce as the Gentlemen choſen

by

by the fea-port Towns; and if not quite clear that the Members for LIVERPOOL and BRISTOL, and the Members for the midland Counties, are equally alive to mercantile interefts, how can you be clear that the " *half of the Houfe who obtain their Seats by* " *purchafe or nomination*," and the half " *elected by the* " *People*," will alike confider *their* caufe and intereft as their own?

It is not, it is not in the nature of things that the fpurious Elections of the Family or Treafury Bo-roughs, fhould anfwer the purpofes of legitimate Reprefentation. The very effence of Reprefentation is gone in him who holds his Seat independent of the Country. What is Reprefentation, or its ufe, if it be not to obtain Legiflators who, feeling the fame interefts, will breathe the fame inclinations and the fame averfions? The Members who proceed from the People are covenanted to take their bent from the People. I afk you, what engagement Legiflators on furreptitious Elections have in common with thofe who are in by real deputation? In the mer-cenary and *pocket* Boroughs, in BARNSTAPLE or MIDHURST, where is the control of the Confti-tuents?—to whom the refponfibility of their Mem-bers? Attentive to private advantage, thefe pfeudo-Reprefentatives, difregarding their diftant and du-bious relation to the People, will ufe their powers as Legiflators to advance their interefts as individuals, at the public expence. On the contrary, preferve the free exercife of the Voters' wills, which would be done by extending, in all cafes, the right of Suf-frage

frage to such numbers, that bribery, or any indirect interposition, could be of no avail; shorten at the same time very confiderably the term of the truft, and the confequent and perpetual connexion between the Delegate and his Conftituents muft preclude finifter conduct.

" *If men*" in every refpect as well " *qualified*" were returned when the elective act is lodged in a ftanding body of thirty, as it is at BATH and EDINBURGH, as if it were devolved on the Inhabitant-Houfeholders— a fluctuating, more numerous, and from thefe caufes no doubt a purer elective affembly—all that I fhould object would be, that the *Corporation* enjoyed what belonged to the *Town*. But where is the man frontlefs enough to fay that Members for Corporate Bodies of the clafs of CHRISTCHURCH or of HARWICH have been, except in matters of Taxation, renowned for their labours of legiflative patriotifm?— Plain men have thought that the infallible way to procure the Election of " *the propereft perfons*," would be fo to regulate Elections, that merit fhould be the fole motive of choice; becaufe when open to venal applications we may confidently predict the fuccefs of a Candidate with no other qualification than the gold in his hand, againft an opponent gifted with every quality to win on the heart.—" *If the propereft perfons* " *were elected*," I would not contend with you that it was of very high moment " *by whom*" they were chofen. Unhappily a reference to the Return-book deftroys your affertion. Search the fucceffive lifts of the Houfe of Commons—you will foon find that the
hereditary

hereditary depravity of Hindon and Stockbridge has not fixed on men quite so eminent for probity and public services as York and Westminster.— Does any one who has not renounced the use of reason associate to the Burgesses of Weobly or Ludgershall, the same ideas of confidence as to the Representors of Surrey or Norfolk ? Or could the public hope of fidelity to the principles of a delegated trust, repose as rationally on the Gentlemen who sit for the Western Boroughs as on the County-Members ? I shall believe the same propensity to exist in the latter to hold themselves released from the obligations of Representatives of the People as in the former, when I believe the same spirit animates the breasts of the Kentish Yeoman and of the clerical candidate for preferment. In fine, is it (I must repeat) a thing to be credited, that the general interest is not more in danger to be sacrificed to private ends where this exalted situation in the State is acquired by men whom the People neither love nor would have trusted, than when given by public affection— a proud distinction, the honorary reward and the proof of superior merit ?

On the cogency of this hypothetical argument you seem to place your main reliance. That it may perplex no one, I will sift it thoroughly; and now let me put it to you in another way. The most pertinacious opposer of a Parliamentary Reform will not hazard the assertion that the assembly acting in the name and on the behalf of the Commonalty of these united Kingdoms, if wholly delegated by the un-

2   bribed

bribed and unbiaffed Suffrages of the People would confift of men with the fame fentiments and purfuits as it now does. I know not whether in your zeal for the Borough-mongers you will deny the unavoidable inference—that the felfith defigns of thofe who procure Seats clandeftinely muft of neceffity differ fo widely from their views who are felected by Electors in fact *worthy and independent*, that who fees not diftinctiy the Vote of the one, muft on many important queftions be diametrically oppofite to what would be the determination of the other?

Perhaps it will be deemed fuperfluous to continue this line of argument further. But you fhall have " a corollary rather than want." I reft it on the common fenfe of mankind whether we can form as fure a judgement of the collective will of the County of WILTS from the Votes of the fubftitutes of the noble Proprietor of OLD SARUM, as from thofe of the Knights of that Shire? And whether experience decide that the former, difcarding individual intereft, " *know and promote the intereft*" of this County as attentively as the latter? In other words, would you infult the afhes of SAWBRIDGE and SAVILE by a comparifon with *** or with ****— Can you degrade the Liverymen of LONDON and the Freeholders of YORKSHIRE to a level with the Potwallopers of SHAFTESBURY and the Burgagors of of PETERSFIELD? Now, as far as other component parts partake of the fame faults, the aggregate muft be faulty, at leaft in a commenfurate degree : as the collective worth of our " *National Reprefentation*" can

refult

refult only from the perfonal worth of the individuals who compofe it. The aggregate muft in exact proportion, if not in a compound ratio, fail to be an organ to collect the public fentiment, and to infure the end and aim of Reprefentation—an *Identity of Intereft* between the People and their appropriate branch of the Legiflature. Attend to the inference to be deduced from this inquiry. It is, that whether we furvey this mafs in the grofs, or fingle out determinate objects, we alike difcern that the character (and by confequence the qualifications and the conduct) of the *Elected*, depends on the character, becaufe on that circumftance depends the choice of the *Electors*. For the future, then, you will not rafhly pronounce that " *it fignifies little who return the* " *national counfellors*" intrufted to " *promote the public* " *intereft*" by enacting Laws to bind the Lives and Birthrights of the People of *Britain*.

It would have furprifed me, if the antiquity of the multifarious rights of voting at Parliamentary Elections had not found a place among your objections to their correction. Be any cuftom repugnant to reafon, or bent from its firft direction, if but old, it will always find defenders. So prone is the human mind to refift change. No fooner is it propofed to rectify an obfolete abfurdity or an immemorial abufe, than the Reformers are fure to be conjured not to innovate with new-fangled refinements the provifions of antient prudence. Then are we ftunned with the bawling of all who are willing to blunder on from generation to generation in error, provided the error

C   be

be prefcriptive. Away with this common-place. Our anceftors did much for us : but no (not your) antipathy to Reform will fay *in pofitive terms*, they left us nothing to do.

Sir, be affured I bear due refpect to " *long* " *eftablifhed, or even fettled rules.*" The difference between us is this—I declare for antient principles— You are tenacious of old forms ; becaufe I admire the theory of the Conftitution, and you approve the practice.—I venerate the age of Parliament, but would transfufe into its debilitated frame a frefh portion of the bloom and vigour of youth. You dote on fuperannuated imbecility, and are enamoured with grey hairs and wrinkles which you fondly fancy it would disfigure the beauty of the Conftitution to remove.—I mean not to deny that every well-wifher to Parliamentary melioration has to regret the departure from many good old " *rules,*" and the fubftitution of their reverfe. For inftance, it was the wholefome ufage of former times, to recur to what I have mentioned already, for the Delegates to be paid by thofe who fent them a pecuniary remuneration for their labours in Parliament. This " *rule*" has been turned quite round. Without looking out of your work we find it has grown up into an avowed practice for numbers " *to purchafe their Seats,*" and Wages, at leaft from their Conftituents, fince the days of MARVEL have been received by none of the Members.—Of old this was the anfwer of the Commons " when any new device is moved on the " King's behalf in Parliament, that they dare not

.   " agree

" agree without conference with their Countries." *
This anfwer has funk into difufe—fo long funk into
difufe that many Members fpurn at the idea of obedience to Inftructions.—In derogation of popular
rights, we continue to fummon *four* Burgeffes from a
decayed hamlet, like EAST LOOE and WEST LOOE,
while we fuffer Towns rifen to the repute of MAN-
CHESTER and SHEFFIELD to be deftitute of a voice in
Parliament. But in Parliaments that are paffed, as
Towns increafed in "trade and grew populous
" they were admitted to a fhare in the Legifla-
" ture."—BLACKST. *Com. v.* 1. *p.* 174. 8*vo.* On the
fame reafon, CALAIS when annexed to the Crown
of England fent Burgeffes to Weftminfter †.—
Thus highly the principle was in better days re-
fpected of affigning feparate agents in Legiflation to
diftricts intitled to them by their importance. We
congratulate ourfelves on the fuperior diffufion of
political knowlege in our own age, yet we leave the
choice of Legiflators with beggary and ruins, and re-

---

* Sir Edw. COKE. 4 Inft. 11.—" Many in all ages, and fome-
" times the whole body of the Commons have refufed to give
" their opinion in fome cafes, till they had confulted with thofe
" who fent them : The Houfes have bin often adjourned to
" give them time to do it ; and if this were done more fre-
" quently, or that the Towns, Citys, and Countys, had on fome
" occafions given Inftructions to their Deputys, matters would
" probably have gone better in Parliament than they have often
" done."—SIDNEY; *Difc. concerning Government. ch.* 3. *fect.* 38.

† WHITELOCKE's *Notes uppon the King's Writt for cheofing
Members of Parlement.* 2. 359.

fufe

fuse this high franchize to wealth and population!
A twofold violation of antient principle. For it is
not only that the sorry place WEYMOUTH stands on
the same footing in our Parliamentary councels with
the Counties of KENT and ESSEX—not merely that
the names of deserted villages, have never been
erazed from the rolls of Parliament, of which the
Reformers complain. They are further shocked by
the joint-existence of contradictory abuses—by the
actual presence in the Parliament-House of Members
for NEWTOWN and GATTON, as well as by the non-
Representation of such flourishing Towns as LEEDS
and BIRMINGHAM.—The time has been that *Sessional*,
not as now septennial Parliaments, were a " *settled*
" *rule.*" That none who were not inhabitants of the
place were eligible was another " *early rule,*" and
" *established*" by positive Statutes. Now, not only
Electors are non-resident, but a Member may be
ignorant of the County where the corn-fields lie for
which he *serves* in Parliament. " In the olden time"
before us, the Exchequer had no character to denote
a million of money, and Aids and Subsidies were
wrung with reluctant murmurs from the parsimonious
Commons. We have lived to see and to feel millions
and tens of millions voted in one Session, and without
the formality of a Division. There was too another
maxim which we should do well to revive. When
money was taken from our forefathers, they felt some
alleviation of their additional burthens in so far as it
was a Custom of Parliament that a redress of Grievances and a grant of Supplies " went hand in hand."

To

To every Money-bill was tacked fome Bill favourable to the People *. Of late, acceffions of Influence
have been their only remuneration. It is now their
misfortune that every increafe of Taxation neceffarily
fwells the Influence of the Crown, while it leffens
the fecurity of the Subject by adding to the numbers, and by inlarging the powers, of Revenue Officers.

To return (if it can be faid I have digreffed), as
you refort to the ftale cant, of refpect for cuftoms,
becaufe handed down to us from high antiquity, I
muft remind you that fince Borough-fpeculations
have proved fo gainful, your " *long eftablifhed and*
" *fettled rules*" are daily and notorioufly narrowed,
or diftorted, or fruftrated. Thus, among many
other evafions, often where the Corporators mono-
polize the franchize of Election, he who once ob-
tains the ruling intereft does not fupply vacancies till
the Corporation, reduced as at MARLBOROUGH, and
BUCKINGHAM, to a handful, is to be eafily managed: then of courfe they are filled up with his
own dependents only, nominating one another in
perpetual fucceffion. Hence very many of thefe
public Magiftracies, of late years, have dwindled
into the appendage of a private family. Can you
fay that thefe *clofe* Boroughs have not departed from

---

* " It hath ever been the Cuftom of Parliaments, by good
" and wholefome Laws to refrefh the Commonwealth in ge-
" neral; yea, and to defcend into the remedies of particular
" Grievances, before any mention made of a Supply."—WAL-
LER; *Works*, p. 400. 4to.

the

the meaning of their Grant?—Or that thefe bodies originally incorporated for purpofes beneficial to the community, but now rankly mifufed, ought not to be disfranchized, and the Election thrown open, as the conftitutional principle of free and popular Election demands? [App. D.] For my part, I readily profefs my inability to difcover wherein the difference to the independency of the Reprefentors of the People confifts, between garbling the Charters of Parliamentary Corporations, as our fecond JAMES attempted, and defeating their intent by thefe illufory artifices.—No lefs exceptionable is the practice in the Burgage-tenure Boroughs, where the right of voting is now holden to be an incident infeparable from certain fpots of ground, from the fites of hovels—from " deferted fhambles, or a gravel-pit*! Thefe, formerly in various hands, have been bought up by fome wealthy individual, who fatisfies the forms and circumftances of an Election by polling his *parchment*-Voters before the ink of their Conveyance be well dry.—He muft indeed be poffeffed with a mechanical habit of admiring antiquated ufages, who knowing that to fend Reprefentatives was originally deemed a *Service*, now hears this common and political right treated as a fpecial *Privilege*, and as vendible *Property*, yet writes about adhering to " *long eftablifhed and fettled rules.*"

Talk no more, Sir, of " *long eftablifhed and fet-* " *tled rules.*" It is idle, unlefs you were able to dif-

---

* See the DOWNTON-Cafe; 1 *Luder's* Rep. of Election-Committees, 162.

prove

prove the taunt of the Foreigner *, were he to addrefs you after this manner—' Your Law vaunts
' that Englifhmen act in Legiflation " either in per-
" fon, or by Reprefentation upon their own free
" Elections." [App. E.] ' Annul this declaration
' which now ftands on your Statute-Book only to
' reproach you. Why the very inhabitants of one
' of the fuburbs of London (the *Tower Ham-*
' *lets*), even prefuming againft the fact, that none
' of your Elections were fuppofititious, outnumber
' the Conftituents of a Majority of your lower
' Houfe of Legiflature. [App. F.] The vocabulary
' of contempt (he might prefume to add) furnifhes
' no name to ftigmatize the fupine indifference of
' the Englifh Nation to the barefaced market of the
' legiflative office. When you cannot deny (he
' might tell us) that Perpetuities and Reverfions of
' Seats, among your Reprefentatives, are advertized
' for fale by auction as publicly as feats at your
' Theatres!' [App. G.]

Such are the frauds on the Law; and such the
innovations on the approved policy of our antient
Conftitution—by means of which a mob of Cour-
tiers and felf-exiftent Members, as well as fhoals of
the nominees of Peers, and of other " *fingle pro-*

---

* " On répète tous les jours dans les pays etrangers que le
" Peuple Anglois n'eft point repréfenté comme il devroit
" l'etre."—" Un des plus grands malheurs de l'Angleterre eft
" en effet que fa Reprefentation Parlementaire foit tres-inegale,
" & l'on peu ajouter, fort *interéfsée à refter tres-inegale*."—
MIRABEAU.

" *prietors*

" *prietors of great estates*," under an arrogated sanc-
tion, croud into and pollute the Houfe of the People.   Reprefentatives merely titular—How much,
how infinitely more pernicious to the Liberties of
England than if *John Doe* and *Richard Roe* had in
fuch cafes been the Return to the Sheriff's Precept
of Election !

LETTER II.

" Could we suppofe a Body politic framed perfect in its firft
" conception or inftitution, yet it muft fall into decays, not
" only from the force of accidents, but even from the very
" ruft of time; and *at certain periods muft be furbifhed up, cr re-*
" *duced to its firft principles, by the appearance and exercife of fome*
" *great virtues, or fome great feverities.*"

Sir W. TEMPLE; *Effay on Popular Difcontents. Works, v.* 1.
p. 258. *fol.*

SIR,

I COME now to an objection againft a **Reform of**
the fophifticated Reprefentation of this country, on
which you feem to lay much ftrefs—that no " *new*
" *fcheme promifes to collect together more wifdom, or*
" *produce firmer integrity*" than that in ufe. If this
pofition be true, your declamation on the neceffity of
Influence to carry forward the bufinefs of the Nation
in Parliament, is pregnant with a melancholy reflection. I fhould be forry to think felfifh depravity to be fo intimately moulded into the heart, that
no modes of Election could " *collect,*" throughout a
population of perhaps ten millions, fufficient " *wif-*
" *dom and integrity,*" though intereft do not clafh
with duty, to affent to the regulations requifite to
the common welfare, unlefs *influenced* by private and
mercenary motives. Holding a more favourable
opinion of our fellow-citizens in particular, and of
our fellow-men in general, I am perfuaded that the
mif-

mifchief originates in thofe imperfections and confequent perverfions of our Reprefentative Syftem which you admire and defend. Let us examine. You intreat us to confider duly that " we *have* a " Houfe of Commons compofed of five hundred " and *forty* [fifty] eight Members, in which num- " ber are to be found *the moft confiderable Landholders* " *and Merchants of the kingdom; the heads of the* " *Army, the Navy, and the Law: the occupiers of* " *great Offices in the State; together with many pri-* " *vate individuals eminent by their knowlege, eloquence,* " *or activity.* Now *if* the country be not fafe in " fuch hands, in whofe may it confide its interefts? " *If* fuch a number of fuch men be liable to the " influence of corrupt motives, what Affembly of " men will be fecure from the fame danger? *Does* " *any new fcheme of Reprefentation promife to collect to-* " *gether more wifdom, or produce firmer integrity?*" " In this view of the fubject, and attending not to " ideas of abftract proportion and regularity (of " which many minds are much enamoured), *but to* " EFFECTS *alone*, we may difcover juft excufes for " thofe parts of the prefent Reprefentation which " appear to *a hafty obferver* moft exceptionable and " abfurd."—P. 488. As in this paffage you feem, Sir, to more than infinuate that fo long as men of thefe denominations be convened to debate on national affairs, it matters not whether they be called to that high office by the unfuborned voice of the People, or be named by a mandatory recommendation of the Crown or its Minifters, perhaps it would

have

have been as well to have " *declined all conference*" with you. However, as this doctrine, wholly repugnant both to the letter and the reason of our limited form of Government, founds as yet harsh and grating in the ear of an Englishman, it was incumbent on you first to prove, *that* the upper ranks of society are endowed with transcendent powers of intellect, superior acquirements, and more inflexible integrity, than lower stations : *That* honours and emoluments, hanging full in the sight of all who aim at the most exalted posts in " *the Army, the Navy,* " *and the Law,*" do not too often dazzle them so much as to turn them aside from the path of rectitude, to gather some of those flowers and fruits in all seasons to be found in the purlieus of a Court : *That* he who is given a place of profit does not varnish his implicit submission to the dictates of his Patron by pleading, ' I must vote as directed ; my ' politics may be wrong, but I cannot be wrong in ' my gratitude :' *That* the choice of the People is blind, falling on men notoriously defective in wisdom and virtue : *That* our forefathers, when with parental anxiety they strove by every preventive regulation which their foresight, in days of simplicity and truth, could devise to guard against all infringements of THE FREEDOM OF ELECTION, and to preserve the honesty of their Representatives when elected, proceeded on groundless apprehensions : *That* therefore, the Clause declaring that ELECTIONS OF MEMBERS OF PARLIAMENT OUGHT TO BE FREE, should be blotted from the BILL OF RIGHTS,

and

and at the fame time every Act vacating the Seats
of Placemen and Penfioners in fome cafes, in others
difqualifying them for fitting in Parliament, fhould
be torn from the Statute-book as injurious. Yes !
Sir, you muft previoufly prove that rank and wealth
announce talents, knowlege, and probity: *That*
honours and emoluments are not infnaring: *That*
perfonal obligations do not warp the mind from
public duties: *That* the People are not competent to
fix on proper guardians of their Liberty and Property: *That* the terrors of our anceftors being falfe,
their precautions to fecure the Freedom of Election, and the Independency of Members of Parliament were pernicious; and, by confequence, *that*
every ftatutory provifion to preferve the INTEGRITY
OF PARLIAMENT fhould be holden to be a dead letter.—Meanwhile you ought not to expect any perfon to acquiefce in your train of reafoning, an Elec-
tion-broker perhaps excepted.—Befide : Grant that
" *no new fcheme of Reprefentation promifes to collect to-*
" *gether more wifdom, or produce firmer integrity.*"
Well; what is the conclufion from " *this view of*
" *the queftion ?*" Indifputably, that there would be
no danger in appeafing the clamour of " *the Re-*
" *formers*" by gratifying their demands. Certainly,
it efcaped you that in putting this queftion you
throw afide all fears that the caufe of Corruption
would fuftain injury through the introduction of
" *more wifdom and integrity*" by equalized Elections.

Let me not be uncandid. Perhaps you did not
wilfully pafs fophiftry on you readers. You might
be

be unaware that (with the fingle exception of Merchants) your impofing defcription of the Commons'
Houfe of Parliament holds equally true applied to
the Houfe of the Peers. That feparate and permanent body comprizes your. colourable criteria of
the beft " *fcheme of collecting wifdom and integrity*"
to regulate ftate-affairs. There too we *have* " *the*
" *moft confiderable Land-holders of the Kingdom, the*
" *heads of the Army, the Navy, and the Law, the*
" *occupiers of great Offices in the State, together with*
" *many private individuals eminent by their knowlege,*
" *eloquence, and activity.*"—Whatever may be the
advantages derived to the mixed nature of our political fyftem, by a titled and hereditary Order, as
a patrician barrier to ftand between the Crown and
the Commons, yet no man, who deferves attention,
will advance that it would be " *fafe*" to refign
" *the country into their hands,*" nor will recommend
it to " *confide its interefts*" folely to them. Moft indifputably the Englifh Conftitution of Government
abhors the fuppofition : otherwife it would not have
inftituted " general Inquifitors of the Realm *," whom
it prefumes to receive their commiffion from the People to confult *circa ardua regni*—to affefs their contributions to the State, to enact Laws, to audit the public
difburfements, to advife the Crown, and to control or
approve the acts of the Minifters of State. Thereby
forbidding us to believe that " *fuch a number of fuch*
" *men*" as you are content to fuppofe adequate to all

---

* Sir Edw. Coke; 4 Inft. 11.

the ends of good Government are NOT " *liable to*
" *the influence of corrupt motives.*"—By your eſtimate, it ſhould appear, that one who aſpires to be
a preceptor of " *Political Philoſophy,*" is ſtill to be
taught that ſomething more than large property,
external eminence, and ſhining talents are requiſite
in an aſſembly of Legiſlators. Theſe qualities will
not, Sir, alone.warrant you in contending that where
they be found, that body is the beſt calculated to
work out public happineſs—Becauſe theſe qualities
do not neceſſarily involve an IDENTITY OF INTEREST
between the *Governed* and their *Governors.*

Hiſtory exhibits (and, ſo long as Self continues
to be the general* and predominant impulſe
of action in Man, every volume will exhibit)
abundant.and indubitable evidence, that among Legiſlators not feeling a Community of Intereſt, all
idea of a public truſt will be loſt in private conſiderations. Diſtinct from the People they invariably
ſet up an intereſt diſtinct from the intereſts of the
People. Where this one thing is wanting, men
have no rational aſſurance that the virtue of their
rulers will be proof againſt the allurements of
power. A *Corporation-ſpirit* abſorbs the character
of a *National Committee*, and the public weal is ſa-
crificed to the " pride of place," the peculations of
avarice, and the luſt of dominion.

This Identity of Intereſt is to be attained by a
participation of the People in their own Govern-

* I ſay *general.* We ſee ſplendid exceptions which prove it
not to be *univerſal.*

ment, [App. H.] and to be attained by that mode
alone. For the People are folely and invariably
actuated by this motive—the good of the whole.
They can have no intereft adverfe or feparate from
general profperity, and therefore never, never have
confpired againft it. But it is impracticable for all
the individuals conftituting a State of any extent of
territory to exprefs their will in perfon. Were it not
fo, promifcuous multitudes are fickle and turbulent;
fometimes fluggifh, and fometimes precipitate. On
many accounts a concourfe of affembled numbers is
unfit to fhare immediately in the fyftematical and
operofe meafures requifite in national proceedings.
This was in former ages the grand *defideratum*—to
contrive fome orderly method of learning and di-
gefting the fenfe of the People *. How to condenfe
public virtue, and to confolidate the gathered wifdom
of a nation, is the noble difcovery of modern Europe
in political fcience. Happily it is no longer pro-
blematical, that thofe functions which the People are
unable to exercife by their fpecial interpofition they
can perform *mediately*—by a *temporary* delegation of
their authority to depofitaries felected from and by
themfelves. The Affemblies of the Eftates under
the Feudal Syftem unfolded, moft probably by
chance, that fuch a devolution of the popular will

* " To follow, not to force the public inclination; to give
" a direction, a form, a technical drefs, and a fpecific fanction,
" to the general fenfe of the community, is the true end of
" Legiflature." BURKE; *Works, v. 2. p.* 136.

combines as great public fpirit as animated the De-
mocracies of Greece or the Roman Republic in their
proudeft æras with the order and ftability of opinion
neceſſary in Councils charged with the weighty
buſineſs of empire. In a Legiſlature of which a juſt
Repreſentation of the People compoſes a conſtituent
part, a real and moſt intimate connection is made to
ſubſiſt between the Legiſlators and the ſubjects of
their Legiſlation. Its Members aſſured, if they ſwerve
from their duty, that they ſhall ſpeedily be refolved
into the common maſs, and muſt on their return to
private life individually bear an equal load of the
grievances they ſhould impoſe, their intereſt muſt be
one and the ſame with that of their Conſtituents :
Therefore it is that an Houſe of Repreſentatives is
the only place where power may be ſecurely repoſed,
and ought not to be dreaded. There it is formidable only to corruption and impoſture. In a
word ; an Aſſembly thus identified with the People,
by inſuring as well frugality in the adminiſtration of
national affairs as the equal bleſſings of Liberty, pro-
vides a ſafeguard that Law ſhall never lapſe into op-
preſſion, nor Taxation be wound up into legalized
rapine.

Theſe are immutable tenets in the civil creed of
our " *Parliamentary Reformers*," and imbibed from
the Conſtitution of the Government under which
they were born. It remains for me, Sir, to bring
them home to our own " buſineſs and boſoms."
There is no need again to have recourſe to your
proſpectus of the corruptions in the Repreſentation.

That

That may be done on higher authority. In the records of Parliament it is clearly articulated, and evidence tendered to verify the facts at the Bar, that " *eighty-four* individuals do by their own immediate " authority fend *one hundred and fifty-feven* Mem- " bers"—and that " *one hundred and fifty* more are " returned by the *recommendation* of *feventy* powerful " individuals—making the total number of Patrons " only *one hundred and fifty-four* who return in the " whole THREE HUNDRED AND SEVEN." [App. I.] A decifive Majority of the Britifh Houfe of Commons!!! More than this—the fame Record empowers me to aver, that in ENGLAND and WALES, (exclufive of SCOTLAND) nearly a MILLION OF HOUSEHOLDERS, paying Taxes, have, as fuch, " no " voice in the Reprefentation."—" Neither their " contributions to the public burthens, their peace- " able demeanour as good Subjects, nor their ge- " neral refpectability and merits as ufeful Citizens, " afford them as the Law now ftands, the fmalleft " pretenfions to participate in the choice of thofe " who *under the name of their Reprefentatives,* may " difpofe of their Fortunes and Liberties." Or rather—for why do I vary your own emphatic illuftration—every fuch non-elector may indeed complain—" *I have no Reprefentative at all, nor any more* " *power or concern in the Election of thofe who make the* " *Laws by which I am governed,* THAN IF I WAS A " SUBJECT OF THE GRAND SEIGNIOR."

When to thefe great and inherent defects in the frame of Parliament we couple its feptennial dura-

tion,

tion, the Lower Houfe, I fear, carries in its prominent features too many infallible tendencies toward
an oligarchical and ftanding SENATE. [App. K.] To
fay no more, it is *not* a Houfe of Commons, renewed
by frequent Elections, wherein every man enjoying
a vifible pledge to fociety exercifes the right of
Suffrage. Where then (it may be afked) is the community of feeling requifite to breed that intereft, one
and indivifible, which forms the diftinctive character
of a Houfe of Legiflature truly reprefentative ? " For
" the foundation's loft of *common good* *," till that
portion of their Reprefentation, now purloined from
the People, be retrieved. If thefe things have not
almoft deftroyed its operation among us, here are
obvious caufes (fay the friends of conftitutional re-
novation) to conclude that its advantages muft be
lamentably diminifhed. And of what are they defirous ?—Of innovations on ENGLISH ideas of Liberty ? No: They adhere to the genuine characteriftic of their own Conftitution. Wherefore it is
their reafonable prayer to be *remitted* to the antient
right of the Englifh Commons—*a Reprefentative in
full,* FREE, *frequent, and* NEW *Parliaments.* They crave
no fanciful alterations. They propofe not to abolifh,
but to reftore and to improve ; where to improve is
to perpetuate. By repairing and widening the bafe,
they would ftrengthen the edifice and perfect its
fymmetry. Full well they know our fyftem contains
within itfelf the power of correction by fafe, regular

* Otway.

and legal means, and they demand no fpeculative nor
extra-conftitutional expedients. Obeying the pre-
cepts of BLACKSTONE, HUME, and many others—
" *Hafty obfervers*" (you think) but furely zealous and
not ignorant fupporters of all the three Eftates in our
Conftitution—the " *Reformers*" of Parliament feek
to enlarge and to invigorate that branch of it, which
from the inceffant alterations in all human affairs,
co-operating with an extenfive change in manners,
in the nature of property, fuper-added to various
political circumftances, they conceive to be grown
inefficient to its original ufes.

You are now, perhaps for the firft time, in full
poffeffion of the elevated grounds on which " the
" Reformers of England" take their ftand. Thence,
you muft difcern their *end* is to banifh all partial and
felfifh views from the manfion of Legiflation, in
order to make room for an infeparable " *fociety of*
" *interefts*." Their *mean* a fair Reprefentation of the
People in a Houfe of Commons *purely elective*. In
that hope, founded on thefe confiderations, it is the
wifh of many to call the Mafters of Families into
political exiftence; a very numerous and the moft
refpectable clafs in fociety, on whom the burthen of
Government heavily and chiefly preffes. This is
the " *fcheme*" they dare to " *premife will collect more*
" *wifdom*," and, by creating a conftant union of
fympathy and fentiment between the Electoral and
the Delegated Bodies, will, they are confident, " *pro-*
" *duce firmer integrity*."—When the happy day arrives
that the one cannot be affected without producing

corre-

correfpondent emotions in the other, the country will never again be driven to make its will known by the circuitous mode and uncertain iffue of County-Meetings and general Affociations—to fet up the voice of the People againft the Vote of the Legifla-ture. We fhall then be fure that no meafure can be carried thro' Parliament that will not be ftamped with the corroborative fanction of national appro-bation.

Far different muft it be while the Borough-holders occupy by fufferance the greater part of the Houfe which of right belongs to the " *national Repre-*" *fentatives."* The fame painful alternative, as in the American War, will continually recur fo long as the fame caufe fhall fubfift. In this predicament the People have only to interpofe their fenfe to the acts of the conftituted power of the State, or to ftand quiefcent fpectators of Minifters and their Majorities running the career to public ruin.

By this time, you perceive that no difguft at the maze in which the right of Parliamentary Suffrage is bewildered prompts thofe to whom I joined my petitionary voice in imploring Parliament to improve its own excellencies. Undoubtedly we wifh to fa-cilitate thefe intricacies; yet our minds are not led away by " *ideas of abftract proportion and regularity,"* as you fuggeft, previoufly to your appeal " *to effects* " *alone."* All enumeration of the " *effects"* on which you fo boldly rely, you have moft unaccountably omitted. However, we gladly accept your chal-lenge, and rejoin that rouzed by " *effects"* to the in-veftigation

vefligation of caufes, before we propounded remedies
we traced the grievances we labour under up to the
objects of our Reform. The motives that impel us
are manifold. But not to take too wide a range,
I will confine myfelf to two points.—The enjoyment
as well of perfonal Freedom as of Property is the
paramount principle of the focial order. The fecurity of the one, and the protection of the other,
then muft be the fupreme objects of folicitude with
every legiflative Affembly properly compacted for
the advancement of public happinefs. You cannot except, if we appretiate our *virtual* Reprefentation by its attention to what is moft dear and valued
among men.

On the firft head, let it fuffice to caft a retro-
fpective glance on the conduct of the Majority when
the legality of General Warrants was brought before
this Houfe early in the prefent reign. Should they
defend from arbitrary feizure our Perfons and Papers
was the queftion? It was the caufe of every clafs of
the People. How peculiarly their care to whom we
fhould look up as the tutelary protectors of our Laws
and Liberties! They refufed to come to a declaratory Vote fo favourable to the conftitutional rights
of their fellow-fubjects! And their acquiefcence in
the adroit fubterfuge to efcape indirectly from the
queftion fills the mind with indignant forrow.—
A few months afterward the Court of King's Bench
adjudged General Warrants to be illegal and void *.

* See Money v. Leach: 3 Burr. Rep. 1742. 1 Blackft. Rep.
555. S. C.

I now

I now pafs to the other head, namely, the protection of Property. Underftand me not to mean that Property is unprotected by our Courts of Law. Far be it from me to mutter a hint of a failure of Juftice between man and man. I advert to revenue-peculation under the pretext of contributions to the public wants. Setting afide parochial and other Rates, before we were again plunged into the abyfs of War, SEVENTEEN NETT MILLIONS OF POUNDS were annually exacted from the People, and after a Peace of nine years, to pay the Intereft of the National Debt *then* accrued, and to defray the current expences of a. *Peace-eftablifhment!* The magnitude of this Debt, and the concomitant extent of Taxation [App. L.]— A Debt exceeding all the gold and filver in the hand of Man, and a yearly Taxation probably fwallowing up the whole of the Coin in circulation, are evidence conclufive in my judgment to prove that " fome-" thing is rotten in the State." Now where can we look, when complaining of a lavifh ufe of public treafure, but to thofe who hold the purfe-ftrings of the Nation ? Is it to be diffembled or eluded that much of this Expenditure, and a large proportion of this Debt muft be pofted to the account of ADMINISTRATION-PARLIAMENTS ? Parliaments *influenced* to fet no ftint to the demands on the public coffers. If the Commons' Houfe, renewed at fhort intervals, had wholly emanated *from* and therefore fully fympathized *with* the main body of the People, would there have been, Parliament after Parliament, the ready refponfive AYE to minifterial requifitions to take the People's money ? [App. M.] That this is

the

the chief fource of the burthens we bear, and may have ftill to dread, it is, I think, difficult to miftake. The more efpecially when we call to mind that in 1716—before Election-brocage had been elaborated to a fyftem, and when an Houfe of Commons deputed for *three* years protracted its own exiftence, and that of future Houfes to *feven*—our Debt amounted but to *fifty-four* millions. Alas! at the clofe of the laft Seffion, funded and unfunded, fuppofing it converted into a three *per cent.* Stock, the Debt exceeded THREE HUNDRED AND EIGHTY-THREE MILLIONS *, and is in a rapid courfe of augmentation.

You muft affign ftrong reafons to unfettle my conviction, the refult (you fee) of inquiry and reflection, that this frightful enhancement is not attributable to the evil principle of undue Influence having fince that period been able to act with increafed, I might fay accelerating vigour. This ufe or abufe of Public Credit by Miniftry after Miniftry practifing on the credulity, or the exceffive complaifance (or what may I call it?) of Parliament, fpeaks for itfelf. It is evidence ever prefent of the " *effects*" naturally generated by your " *Government of Influence*," and an enervated Reprefentation †.

---

* See MORGAN's Supplement to a Review of Dr. PRICE's Writings on the Finances of Great Britain. *p.* 9. Cadell. 1795.

† " A frugal adminiftration of the public treafure is a fign of " a well-governed State, which can never be well governed " where the public treafure is wafted and mifapplied." *The Works of Tacitus, with Political Difcourfes ; by* T. GORDON, *v.* 5, *p.* 58. 12mo.

It will be no anſwer to reply that we enjoy many bleſſings under the exiſting regimen. Many and great let them be. All the privileges yet remaining to diſtinguiſh us from the other Nations of Europe are referable to the portion the People have poſſeſſed in their own Government by Repreſentation, imperfect as that Repreſentation has now grown. The People have theſe benefits not *becauſe* they have little (as ſome with unparalleled effrontery aſſert) but *altho'* they have little political power. The true queſtion ſtill continues unanſwered—whether a ſyſtem which has mortgaged the landed Rental of the whole Iſland, and entailed ſuch enormous burthens on us and our poſterity, do not call aloud for amendment ſomewhere? And it is ſtill open for thoſe who think with me that *that* amendment muſt be in our defective Repreſentation to aſk, as Mr. PITT when a Reformer aſked, " if there always had been an " Houſe of Commons who were the faithful ſtewards " of the intereſts of their country, *the diligent checks* " *on the adminiſtration of the Finances,* the conſtitutional " adviſers of the executive branch of the Legiſla- " ture, the ſteady and *uninfluenced* friends of the " People, WOULD THE BURTHENS WHICH THE CON- " STITUENTS OF THAT HOUSE WERE NOW DOOMED " TO ENDURE HAVE BEEN INCURRED?"—*See De- brett's Parliamentary Regiſter,* v. 18. p. 49.——

" Whatever (you continue to obſerve) may be the " defects of the preſent arrangement, it infallibly " ſecures a great weight of property to the Houſe of " Commons, by rendering many Seats in that Houſe " acceſſible to men of large fortunes, and to thoſe alone—

" by

" by which means fuch men are engaged in the
" defence of the feparate rights and interefts of this
" branch of the Legiflature as are beft able to fup-
" port its claims. The conftitution of *moft of the*
" *fmall Boroughs,* efpecially the Burgage-tenure,
" though not formed with this defign, contributes to
" the fame effect ; for the appointment of the *Repre-*
" *fentatives* we find commonly *annexed to certain*
" *great inheritances."* p. 489.

No doubt the ruinous cofts of contefted Elections as at prefent conducted, throws many of them
into their power who poffefs the deepeft purfe.
Surely Returns procured to Parliament by bearing
down rival Candidates thro' dint of money, with a
number of Boroughs befide ingroffed by the great
Families and by opulent individuals, directly leads in
your own phrafe, to " *a confufed and ill-digefted*
" *Oligarchy."* An evil it behoves us no lefs to
avert than incroachments from any other quarter.
For what would be the character of this Oligarchy of
Borough-mongers both monied and titled ? What
but that of a *fourth* Eftate in the realm, enabled by
the ufurpation of our elective rights, to bully their
King and to domineer over the People ? Through a
fingular infatuation, we fhould then have " facri-
" ficed Liberty to a fcrupulous adherence to thofe
" forms and maxims which were originally efta-
" blifhed to preferve it."—In a topic of the magnitude of that we now agitate, it is not worth while
to altercate on your enormous folecifm in terms—
" *hereditary Reprefentation !"* I cannot however dif-

miss it without confessing my eagerness to hear, by
what process an elective and temporary office (conferred on the individual, not for his own emolument,
but in trust for the public benefit) can be transmuted
into an absolute estate of inheritance without impair-
ing its functions?

" When *Boroughs are set to sale*, those men are
" likely to become purchasers, who are enabled by
" their talents *to make the best of their bargain.*" p. 489.
—Strange language, Sir, if by. " *make the best of their*
" *bargain*" you mean advance the public good. Sure
I am, this wish never induced any one to " *purchase*"
a Seat in Parliament. *Non hæc in fœdera.* They who
buy will sell.

" *When Boroughs are set to sale!*" With what
indignant surprise would the venerable MAYNARD,
the virtuous SOMERS, and the illustrious band who
stood forward at the expulsion of the *Tarquin* race of
STUARTS—with what indignant surprise would they
have started at this expression ! It is not for me to
undertake to delineate what would have been their
emotions at the remainder of your sentence. Often
have writers deplored " the evil days" on which
it was their lot to have fallen. To vindicate the de-
generacy of the times, was a novelty reserved for
your moral pen !

Ordinarily, " *the best of the bargain*" has been
jobs *; and while we endure the present system of
Election;

* I was gratified by finding this opinion confirmed by a Reformer of very high rank, and a great authority. On the expediency

Election, parties of all defignations muft do the fame. To retain power their great bufinefs muft be to provide a ftore fufficient to anfwer the demands of thofe who poffefs Borough-intereft.

Another part of this " *bargain*" is Bribery. Its conftant attendant I am willing to fuppofe you overlooked; I mean Perjury. Perjury, of which Election-oaths are the main fource, and Cuftom-houfe and Excife-oaths the tributary ftreams, is now fwollen to a torrent which threatens to fweep away all diftinction between right and wrong. After oaths are debafed into matters of form is it reafonable to wonder that their fanctity in the minds of many no more infpires religious awe ? [App. N.] Stripped of their folemnity, they ceafe to be unerring tefts for the difcovery of truth ; fo that all endeavours at the difpenfation of Juftice too often prove vain. This fearful inundation of Perjury breaks over every mound of Law that Society can erect to protect Property, Life and Reputation. It is an idle hope that it can be effectually checked while the Huftings from *Caithnefs* to *Cornwall* are fuffered to refound with Perjuries—While the Candidates and Electors, the fons of the Duke and the Chimney-fweeper who boils a pot, have their confciences fteeled by thefe execrable electioneering practices. *Abeunt ftudia in mores.*

pediency of the Nation redeeming the proprietary Boroughs, the DUKE OF RICHMOND remarked, that " the Liberties of a " Nation cannot be bought too dear ; but *the whole coft of* " *thefe Boroughs would not amount to the profits of* ONE JOBBING " CONTRACT."—See his Grace's exculpatory evidence on the *Trial of Thomas* HARDY. *v.* 4. *p.* 14.—*Gurney's edit.*

mores. It muſt be an idle hope when Dignitares of the eſtabliſhed Church miſemploy their " heaven-devoted hours" to gloſs with accommodating ſalvoes this diſregard of the religion of an oath in order " *to make the beſt of ſuch bargains.*"

In vain do you pretend, that " when a Seat is no " ſold, but given by the opulent Proprietor of a " Burgage-tenure, the Patron finds his own intereſt " conſulted by the reputation and abilities of the " Member whom he nominates." *p.* 489.—How "*the " Patron finds his own intereſt conſulted*" in the diſpoſal of Seats is much more ſatisfactorily explained by DODDINGTON in his *Diary*; and DODDINGTON you muſt admit is a ſtriking inſtance of your " *con-" ſiderable Landholder, a great officer in the State, " eminent by his knowledge, eloquence and activity*;"—who deſerting his old maſter for greater expectations, from the ſon, might, like the crafty ſtateſman of old, after a ſimilar diſappointment, " have got him home " and hanged himſelf," had he not commanded *ſix* dead Votes in Parliament.—" I muſt think (DOD-" DINGTON obſerves) that ſo much offered and ſo " little aſked, in ſuch hands as theirs (the *Pelhams*) " and at a time when *Boroughs were a commodity " particularly marketable,* could not fail of removing " at leaſt reſentments and of obtaining pardon." *p.* 257. 3d *edit.* And afterward; " I believe (ſays this " right honourable Borough-jobber) there were few " who could give his Majeſty SIX MEMBERS FOR " NOTHING." *p.* 282. Again; " Mr. Pelham declared that I had a good deal of MARKETABLE " WARE

" WARE (Parliamentary intereft) and that if I would
" empower him to *offer it all to the King*, without
" conditions, he would be anfwerable *to bring the*
" *affair to a good account.*" *p.* 308. Elfewhere in this
moft curious and inftructive Diary, it appears that
the affair was the Treafurerfhip of the Navy, a
place of vaft emolument, as the price of the Members he put into Parliament. *Vulgato imperii ar-*
cano !

  " If certain of the Nobility (you fubjoin) hold the
" appointment of fome part of the Houfe of Com-
" mons, *it ferves to maintain that alliance between the*
" *two branches of the Legiflature,* which no good
" Citizen would wifh to fee diffevered ; *it helps to*
" *keep the Government of the country in the Houfe of*
" *Commons, in which it would not perhaps long continue*
" *to refide,* if fo powerful and wealthy a part of the
" Nation as the Peerage compofe were excluded
" from all fhare. and intereft in its conftitution."
p. 490.—That it is prudent for the Commons to.
connive at, and of courfe to concur in, the interference of the Lords of Parliament in their Elections
is too vifionary to need a ferious refutation. But
your defence of what the Houfe themfelves at the.
commencement of their Seffion always refolve to be
" an high infringement upon the Liberties and Pri-
" veleges of the Commons of Great Britain,"
[App. O:] and your defire to palliate the degrada-
tion of the Reprefentatives of the Englifh People
into proxies of the Peers, fhall not be paffed over
without fuitable animadverfion. When the Nobility
were,

were, by the number of their retainers and partizans, much more powerful than in our days, what ftand, Sir, did they make, though leagued with CHARLES, againft the People ?—Fearful of change, fome timid minds difincline to any modification of the elective powers anew, though they acknowlege and deplore the complication of public mifchiefs which enfue from the fubfifting errors. *You* enter the lifts alone, the hardy champion of the " *appoint-* " *ment of part of the Houfe of Commons by the* " *Nobility.*" * To all who reflect that the exiftence and the value of this Conftitution depends on preferving the equipoize between the three Eftates, fuch ufurpation, prefents ample ground of alarm. As " America was faid to be conquered in Ger " many," fo we may fear, if your opinion gain currency, and things fhould continue to run on in the prefent channel, that the independency of the Commons' Houfe may, in after-times, be fubdued in the Houfe of the Lords. *Homines per honores ferire* is an old ftratagem in politics ; perhaps it has not yet grown quite obfolete. What if it fhould ever ripen into a Court-maxim, that the moft meritorious fervice the Commoner, who fighs for a Coronet, can

urge

* On this queftion even SAM. JOHNSO writes thus : " The " ufurpation of the Nobility, for they apparently ufurp all the " influence they gain by fraud, and mifreprefentation ; I think " it certainly lawful, perhaps your duty to refift. What is not " their own they have only by robbery."

urge is, that he has filched a Borough from the
People! Before thefe dealers can " *make the beft*
" *of their bargain*" by this fort of traffic in " mark-
" etable ware," they muft trample on the land-
marks which our fathers fet up to fix the refpective
boundaries of the two Houfes. Recollect that thefe
" *two branches of the Legiflature*" have not co-ordi-
nate functions—That they have diftinct and difcordant duties caft on them. If there be points in the
Law and Cuftom of Parliament better afcertained,
and of greater importance than any other, they are,
1. The exclufive privilege of the Commons to grant
Supplies. 2. Their right, as the grand Inqueft of
the Nation, to prefer articles of Impeachment
againft ftate-criminals. To what end, does their
proper Houfe fpurn every Bill drawing money in any
fhape from the People, when remanded from the
Lords' Houfe with amendments the moft trivial—if
it were not as indifpenfable that Peers fhould not by
their creatures below be parties to framing Money-
bills? And it would be a mockery of Juftice, too
grofs for aggravation, if at any time a prifoner at
the Bar of the High Court of Parliament could
challenge his accufers for the caufe that they were
appointed by his Judges. You could not dip into
political difquifition and remain ignorant of thefe
things, but you would lead us to confound the great
outlines of our Conftitution.—Before you publifh
another impreffion, I entreat you to reflect again
and again whether the admiffion of fo " *powerful*
" *and wealthy a part of the Nation as*" the taxed

Householders to an active "*share and interest in the* "*constitution of the House of Commons*," would not conduce more to its respectability than for "*the* "*Nobility*" in defiance of its Seffional Refolutions "*to hold the appointment of any part.*"

You then afk "where would be the *impropriety* "*or the inconveniency, if the King at once should no-* "*minate* a limited number of his fervants to Seats "in Parliament?"—P. 490. The fame caufes ever produce the fame effects. The "*King nominates*" the twenty-fix Spiritual Lords in the Upper Houfe. The confequence is inevitable. Obedient to the wifh of the Court, in the laft century all the Bifhops, except three, voted *against* the Bill fent up by the Commons to exclude a Popifh fucceffor to the Crown! and twenty-four of the epifcopal Bench perfifted to the laft, as appears by public papers, in fupporting the American War—" That æra of ca- "lamity, difgrace and downfal; an æra which no "feeling mind will ever mention without a tear for "England"—Whereas a large Majority of the Knights of the Shires, now almoft our only confti- tutional Members, long and frequently declared againft it.

"*Where would be the impropriety, if the King no-* "*minate a limited number to Seats?*" Sir, I rebut your queftion by afking, in return, what bias will cleave to Confervators of the Rights of the People nominated by the Crown? And what it is reafon- able to expect from men appointed by the very power the acts of whofe agents they ought to fcan

with

with the ftricteft fcrutiny, and their encroachments to withftand with anxious apprehenfion ?—At once the fervant of the Crown, and the Reprefentor of the People ! It is not eafy to conceive the union of thefe diffonant characters, the Courtier and the Patriot. Could they exercife an independent vote ? They would be without the leaft degree of will ; or for what reafon is every Member, whom the ardour of debate may hurry into an inadvertent mention of the King's name, inftantly called to order ? For what reafon, but that from this quarter folicitations bear the authority of commands ? They would be affembled 'not to deliberate but to approve ; while under other names they might draw private advantage from general calamity. No faith, not fufficiently capacious to digeft a legendary tale, but muft reject the idea that thefe *faithful Commons* would not be " *obliged**" to ratify by their voices whatever was prefcribed.—With divided fervices how could they difcharge the offices of a Reprefentative, and at the fame time fatisfy their employer ?

After you have thus, Sir, vainly ftrove to reconcile us to an Houfe of Commons, HALF of which you ftate to be illegally and unconftitutionally chofen,

---

* " If a father or a mafter, any great benefactor, or one on " whom my fortune depends, require my Vote, *I give it him of* " *courfe*; and my anfwer to all who afk me why I voted fo and " fo, is, that my father, or my mafter *obliged* me: that *I had* " *received fo many favours from*, or had *fo great a dependence* " *upon fuch a one, that I was obliged to vote as he directed me.*" PALEY. *p.* 50.

you

you only touch curforily on " *contracting the duration* " *of Parliament.*" A recurrence to TRIENNIAL ELECTIONS, which would cherifh the vital principles of the Conftitution, as re-animated after the ever-memorable Revolution, you do not blame. Yet we cannot conftrue this filence to mean approbation. —Allow me further to obferve, that a cloiftered Politician, like yourfelf, who employs his induftry to perfuade the People to fet the exterior of their Conftitution above its effentials, ought to be told, and to keep frefh in his memory, the Remonftrance which the firft public body in the Kingdom, after the Houfes of Parliament, but a few years ago carried to the Throne in its corporate capacity. " The " forms of the Conftitution," truly faid " *the good* " *Citizens*" of the Metropolis—" the forms of the " Conftitution, like thofe of Religion, WERE NOT " ESTABLISHED FOR THE FORM'S SAKE, BUT FOR " THE SUBSTANCE; and we call GOD and Men to " witnefs, that as we do not owe our Liberty to " *thofe nice and fubtile diftinctions, which Places, Pen-* " *fions, and lucrative Employments have invented;* fo " neither will we be deprived of it by them; but " as it was gained by the ftern virtue of our an- " ceftors, by the virtue of their defcendants it fhall " be preferved *."

---

* Addrefs, Remonftrance, and Petition of the Lord Mayor, Aldermen, and Livery, of the City of LONDON in Common Hall affembled, to the KING, March, 1770.

LET-

LETTER III.

" The Supreme Executor acts contrary to his trust, when *he*
" *either employs the force, treasure or offices of the Society to corrupt*
" *the Representatives, and gain them to his purposes; or openly pre-*
" *engages the Electors and prescribes to their choice,* such whom he
" has by solicitations, threats, promises, or otherwise, won to
" his designs; and employs them to bring in such, who have
" promised beforehand what to vote, and what to enact. Thus
" to regulate Candidates and Electors, and new-model the
" way of Election, *what is it but to cut up the Government by the*
" *roots, and poison the very fountain of public security* *? For the
" People having reserved to themselves the choice of their Re-
" presentatives, AS THE FENCE TO THEIR PROPERTIES,
" could do it for no other end, but that *they might always be*
" *freely chosen, and so chosen freely act, and advise as the necessity*
" *of the Commonwealth, and the public good, should, upon examina-*
" *tion, and mature debate be judged to require.*"—LOCKE; *of Civil*
Government; Works. v. 2. *p.* 302. *4to.*

SIR,

YOU have compiled a bulky Quarto to inforce a
strict observance of the moral duties in the commerce of domestic society. Among other devices,
you have graduated a moral barometer to ascertain
the various degrees of guilt contracted by the va-

---

* It is worthy of remark that LOCKE caught this metaphor from Sir *Edw.*
COKE, who introduces it with the same application.—" Thomas Long gave the
" Maior of Westbury four pound to be elected Burgesse, who thereupon was
" elected. This matter was examined and adjudged in the House of Commons,
" *secundum consuetudinem Parliamenti,* and the Maior fined and imprisoned, and
" Long removed: *for this corrupt dealing was to poyson the very fountain itself.*"
—4 *Inst.* 23.

rious

rious ſtages of inebriety. [App. P.] Why, inſtead
of bringing the ſame auſterity of doctrine into the
civil relations of life, your ſtate-morality ſhould
relax ſo much as to exculpate Legiſlators.in carrying their powers to market, in ſelling their duty for
perſonal gratifications, I am at a loſs to diſcover.
Was it that there would have been no latitude left
for the operation of Influence? For if you had not
diſpenſed with their obligations, by a neceſſary con-
ſequence, you muſt have rigidly reprehended all
Parliamentary venality. Conſider, public virtue and
private morality are nearly al'ied. A general laxity
in *this* cannot fail to operate powerfully on the national manners in *that* particular *. This proſtitu-
tion of the legiſlative office no caſuiſtical dexterity
in ſplitting a hair can diſtinguiſh from immorality.
Is it not beyond doubt or controverſy culpable, and
an heinous breach of moral fitneſs to require a gra-
tuity not to croſs meaſures of general utility? So
it would be in the caſe of any individual in a private ſtation. How greatly the moral turpitude is
aggravated in an " Attorney for the People," who
ſtands bounden and accountable to them for the
faithful diſcharge of this moſt ſacred of truſts, none
can refuſe to acknowledge. Aſſuredly then your
Parliamentary Ethics are no leſs immoral in princi-

---

* The Gentlemen of the Yorkſhire Committee thought ſuch
practices ſubverſive of Morals, and exhorted all " reſolutely to
" oppoſe that ſyſtem of Parliamentary Corruption, which is
" alike *the bane of national Morality*, and the ruin of public Li-
" berty."—WYVILL's *Political Papers*; v. 2. p. 14.

ple

ple than (I fhall prove them to be) pernicious in
practice.— Your defence of the Influence of the
Crown on Parliament, without which, according to
the continued tenour of your effay, the national bufinefs would be thrown out, from the internal evidence we may be fure fprings from the fame defpotic notion as the cuftom prevalent throughout
the Eaft. Like your politico-moral Cafuiftry, the
delufive logic of thofe inflaved nations affumes that
there is no obligation to execute the duties of an
official truft, unlefs fpecially fee'd : accordingly, in
thofe countries even the fuitors for Juftice never apply to their Judges with an empty hand.

After the indulgence you grant to Parliamentary
Corruption, when foftened into the milder term of
" *Influence*," none could imagine you were ferious
where you fpeak of " *a direct reduction of the pa-*
" *tronage of the Crown*," though you had not in-
cautioufly let drop the veil fo far as to difclofe a
glimpfe of your covert defign by faying, " but
" while we difpute concerning different fchemes of
" Reformation, all directed to the fame end [a di-
" minution of the Influence of the Crown] a pre-
" vious doubt occurs in the debate, *whether the end*
" *itfelf be good, or even* INNOCENT—*whether the In-*
" *fluence fo loudly complained of can be deftroyed or*
" *even diminifhed with fafety to the State.*"—P. 491.
By the word *innocent*, you betray an evident predi-
lection for the indefeazible divine right of Kings, and
the " bowftring maxim" of the paffive obedience of
Subjects, however you may elfewhere oftentatioufly

dif-

disclaim these pestilent delusions. None but a dis-
ciple of Filmer, and this is not the only mark of
your affinity, would attach *guilt* on the thirty Counties, on the Capital, and on many other of the Cities and principal Towns in the Island, who in 1780,
called loudly for a retrenchment in the expenditure
of public money, and other accessary regulations,
to restore to the People the Freedom of Parliament
by a reduction of what they justly termed " THE
" GREAT AND UNCONSTITUTIONAL INFLUENCE OF
" THE CROWN." [App. Q.] Guilt, which if credit
be given to your effusions, was then incurred by more
than one hundred thousand Petitioners and Associa-
tors, who believed that for their exertions they
merited the praise and the thanks of their country.
This is not all—the sequel of this national effort to
decrease the funds of Corruption can be no less re-
prehensible. I allude to the death-bed confession (I
do not say expiatory repentance) of the *American
War* Parliament. The House of Commons who
resolved, " That *it is necessary to declare that the
" Influence of the Crown hath increased, is increasing,
" and ought to be diminished*,*" cannot stand " *inno-
" cent*" in your eyes.

Here, let every of your readers pause to revolve,
that having in an unwary moment exposed in language too obvious for misapprehension, and too ex-
plicit to be explained away, your hidden purpose of
insinuating doctrines subversive of the *principles* of

* 6 Ap. 1780. *Jour. Com.* v. 37. *p.* 763.

our free Conftitution, in your *fecond* edition you fub-
ftituted "*fafe*," for the expreffive word "*innocent*,"
tho' thereby the laft member of your period is ren-
dered tautological and unmeaning*.   On your
amended judgment, you deemed it, Sir, more prudent to refort to your phantom "*danger*" to fcare
us, than it was to conjure up in the broad daylight
of the eighteenth century the chimeras of Prieft-
craft—Illufions only terrible while they hovered in
the gloom of ignorance and monkifh fuperftition,
" when Reafon hylt herfelfe in cloudes of nyghte."

" Were the meafures of *Government* (fay you) op-
" pofed from nothing but principle, *Government*
" ought to have nothing but the rectitude of its
" meafures to fupport *them*; but fince *oppofition*
" fprings from other motives, *Government* muft
" poffefs an Influence to counteract that *oppofition*—
" *to produce not a bias of the paffions, but a neu-*
" *trality!*" *p.* 492.—Your hope to *neutralize* the de-
mocratic acid of Reprefentation with the *alkali* of
regal Influence, and yet to preferve its effential properties uninjured vanifhes on the experiment, as I
am about to prove.   But your abufe of the word

---

* In the *fecond* and in fubfequent editions the paffage runs
thus : " whether the end itfelf be good, or *fafe*—whether the
" Influence fo loudly complained of can be deftroyed, or even
" diminifhed *without danger* to the State," *p.* 491.   Why in ftill
later editions do you fay " *much* diminifhed ?"   By thefe retrac-
tions it fhould feem you are fully confcious that you had over-
fhot yourfelf.   Or has fome friend kindly told you fo?

Govern-

Government calls for some previous remark. You avail yourself of its ambiguity as in vulgar use. By this word, in its correct acceptation, we intend the *plan* of civil polity established in any country. You confound it with the *administration* by the executive authorities—Willing, after the fashion of other courtly writers, to impute a want of confidence in the projects of the Ministry for the time being, to disaffection to the Constitution itself *. Thus much may serve to show your verbal accuracy. But whenever *Government*, in your restricted sense, bring forward propositions embracing the welfare of the State, they never would be rejected by an House of Commons fairly deputed by popular Suffrage. How requisite foever Influence may be in a Legislative Assembly constituted in a way so miserably degenerate as that you advise us to persist in, I am bold to say that the clamours of a contentious systematic " Op-" position" would be as little attended to among real Representatives as they are in a Vestry or Common-Council. Not, Sir, that your reasoning is in this respect at all inconsistent: First, you insist on the expediency of adhering to a scheme of Election by which at least one HALF of the House of Commons (you confess) is illegally and unconstitutionally created. Afterward, naturally enough, you descant on the necessity of Influence to bribe a Legislature

---

* " Under this pompous name of *Government*, will nothing " but the paultry interest, or humour, of the Minister be " couched." BOLINGBROKE ; *Ded. to Differtation on Parties.*

thus

thus packed by means equally venal with fuch an end to defpatch the national bufinefs. You would perfevere in errors that you may juftify abufes. Errors and abufes moving in a circle, and mutually productive and reproductive of each other. To do you juftice, fo far you argue with perfect accuracy. We are agreed, that Members who buy their Seats will thwart every propofition till they have " *made the beft of their bargain*" to reimburfe their Election expences, by ftipulating for a fhare of the bounty difpenfed by the Crown. But what could induce men whom the fpontaneous voice of their fellow-citizens has fent to the chamber of Le-giflation not to lend their concurrence to every meafure calculated for the common advantage? Whence thefe alarms about reviving the dormant principle of the independency of Parliament? From what has been we are to collect what will be. You fhould have given your readers a reference to fome pages of our Parliamentary Hiftory in proof that Members returned by the Election of the People have refufed their confent from factious views*. You were unable to find any fuch cafe; for I fhall

prefently

---

* " The granting of money is the only cafe, where we can
" fuppofe the Members generally engaged by their private
" intereft, to oppofe what is neceffary for the public fervice.
" But this intereft is fo fmall with regard to each particular
" Member that it can never be of any weight. This is demon-
" ftrated, Sir, from the whole courfe of our hiftory : for I defy
" any man to give me an inftance, where the Parliament de-
" nied granting what was neceffary for the public fervice, unlefs
" they were denied juftice with regard to the redrefs of griev-
" ances,

prefently have occafion to remark that you are
driven to take refuge in the wilds of conjecture.
Why then they to whom the adminiftration of the
active powers of Government is committed would
never, acting with honeft views, feel themfelves
diftreffed by the advice and infpection of the independent Reprefentatives of independent Electors,
and you will hardly fay that with other intentions
they fhould be fupported at all. Of one thing we
might be fatisfied, the independent Reprefentatives
of independent Electors would never abandon us
to the ambition of a Minifter, or the pique of a
King. On the other hand, this Influence is capable
of being employed to dreadful purpofes. What
furety have we that a faction may not, hereafter, gain
the afcendancy in the direction of affairs, and the
perfonal aggrandizement of a cabinet-cabal be fet
before the fafety of the Empire ? *Suppofe* an im-
perative Influence fhould quafh by the previous
Queftion every endeavour at inquiry. RESPONSI-
BILITY finks to an empty found whenever the Parliament is prompt to fufpend on *Confidence* its capacity
of fuperintendence and controlment.

But enough! Now to fuppofe your terrors
realized—that we *had* an Houfe of Commons wild
and infamous enough " to obftruct the conduct of
" public affairs by a *wanton and perverfe oppofition.*"

" ances, or unlefs they had well-grounded apprehenfions that
" the money would be mifapplied."—Lord Strange on Mr.
Cornwall's Motion in 1742 for excluding Placemen and Penfioners. See *the Hiftory and Proceedings of the Houfe of Commons.*

p. 492.—In this conjuncture you are not to be told, that the Crown poffeffes an obvious remedy. It can and does diffolve an Affembly fo flagitioufly refractory. The Country, on the contrary, tho' they fhould find the Parliament debauched by Influence, and countenancing the moft ruinous fchemes of a Court, may be condemned to wait till *the feven* years are elapfed. A period which political arithmeticians have found to be equal to *one half* of the probable expectation of human life, taken at the moft favourable age.

With regard to your obfervation that " before the " acceffion of JAMES the firft; or at leaft during the " reigns of his three immediate predeceffors, the " Government of England was *a Government by* " *force*, that is, the King carried his meafures " *by intimidation.*" p. 493—We may fafely affert that our prefent civil eftablifhment is no more connected with the ftretches of power, under colour of Prerogative, antecedent to the Revolution of 1688, than it is with the favage edicts of the Norman invader. If attempts muft be made to break the fpirit of Englifhmen—if we muft either be awed by Prerogative, or be inveigled by Influence, doubtlefs our forefathers made an ill exchange for us. *Prerogative alarms when it attacks.* It becomes us therefore to be well advifed whether it be not better to face this open enemy rather than to prefer the infidious overtures of Influence, which, inftead of rouzing the centinels, feduces them treacheroufly to furrender the garrifon.—A ftrong fenfe of recent

2   danger

danger actuated our anceftors to repair the breaches made in the Conftitution by Prerogative, and to throw up frefh bulwarks againft it. They left us a fortrefs impregnable to all affaults in future. Happy would it have been for their children had they been fkilled fufficiently to countermine a plan of attack, mafked under eftablifhed formalities, by fapping the foundations to the centre, while the furface remains intire. *

Natural Philofphy imparts that the apparent diffolution of a fub.tance is no more than its reproduction in a different fhape. Something analogous you hold to take place in the political world. " After " the Reftoration (you go on to fay) there fuc- " ceeded in its place, and *fince the Revolution has* " *been methodically purfued,* THE MORE SUCCESSFUL " EXPEDIENT OF INFLUENCE. Now we remember " what paffed between the *lofs of terror* and the efta- " blifhment of Influence." p. 493.—It has been received as a maxim, that it is in the nature of bad princes to deal out honours, and lavifh their largeffes with a prodigal hand ; whereas good princes knowing themfelves to reign in the hearts of the People, are invariably fparing in the diftribution of titles, and frugal in their donatives. The juftnefs of this rule will be illuftrated, and the complexion of your admired fyftem of Influence difplayed in native

* " The ftate of things is much altered in this country, fince " it was neceffary to protect our Reprefentatives againft the " direct power of the Crown. *We have nothing to apprehend from* " *Prerogative,* BUT EVERY THING FROM UNDUE INFLU- " ENCE." JUNIUS.

colours,

colours, by tracing, though but flightly, its rife and progrefs.

The infamy of this invention to make the will and pleafure of the Prince the meafure of executive Government, and the real fource of Law, * by con - ciliating with favours when he had not the ftrength to intimidate, belongs to the eleventh Louis. This royal ruffian, *Nerone ipfo Neronior*, was bent on de- livering the Crown from Wardfhip †—for fo he chofe to ftyle the lawful control of the Affembly of the States—and he compaffed his aim by the nefarious refource you defend. Liften to a witnefs above exception. Dr. Robertson informs the world, that this gloomy tyrant " was the firft monarch in Europe " who difcovered the method of managing thofe " great Affemblies, in which the Feudal policy had " vefted the power of granting Subfidies, and of " impofing taxes. *He firft taught other Princes the* " *fatal art of beginning their attack on public Liberty,* " *by corrupting the fource from which it fhould flow.* " *By exerting all his power and addrefs in influencing* " *the Election of Reprefentatives, by bribing or over-* " *awing the Members,* and by various changes which " he artfully made in the form of their deliberations; " Louis acquired fuch entire direction of thefe " Affemblies, that *from being the vigilant guardians* " *of the privileges and property of the People, he ren-* " *dered them tamely fubfervient, in promoting the moft* " *odious meafures of his reign.*"—(*The Hiftory of the*

* Cuncta Legum & Magiftratuum in fe trahens Princeps.

† Mettre le Roy hors de page.

Reign

Reign of the Emperor Charles V. v. 1. p. 100. 4to.)
That this dark and crooked policy, dates its origin
among us from the " *Reftoration*" of the profli-
gate CHARLES, is moft certain. In the fame fpirit,
this *Stuart* tranfplanted hither many other fcandalous
practices and opinions acquired in the court of the
defpot, where he fpent his early life. [App. R.]—
The introduction of thefe fhameful *artes et inftru-
menta regni* forms a memorable epocha in the annals
of Parliament; and I now place againft the praife
of a Collegian, the condemnatory judgement of an
honeft and enlightened Statefman.   When newly
tried, the Chancellor HYDE improbated thefe golden
philtres to excite the illicit affections of Parliament.
He would have the Members under no Influence but
that of " Reafon and Policy."   He indeed was a
fupporter of the Conftitution, not the partizan of
" *Government*."   In oppofition to thofe who laboured
to remove every obftacle to the plots of the reigning
King, who panted after arbitrary power, this faithful follower of his fortunes in their reverfe, coun-
felled him to govern on the plain and open *Englifh*
" Principles of Honour and Wifdom, which had
" hitherto fwayed the Houfe in all matters of
" public concernment."—CLARENDON is no light
authority, and I muft cite the paffage at length
where he lafhes with much feverity your falfe fubfti-
tute for " Reafon and Policy," for " Honour and
" Wifdom."   This great and good man would not
let this novel device of his cotemporaries to curb the
free fpirit of Parliaments defcend to pofterity, unat-
tended

tended by his exculpation. He arraigns " the chief
" men of the Court," becaufe they " took more pains
" to ingratiate themfelves than to advance the in-
" tereſt of their mafter ; and *inſtead of preſſing what*
" *was deſirable upon the ſtrength of Reaſon and Policy,*
" *as they had uſed to do, and by which the major part*
" *of the Houſe had uſually concurred with them,* they
" now applied themſelves with addrefs to thoſe who
" had always frowardly oppoſed whatſoever they
" thought would be grateful to the King : and de-
" fired rather to *buy their Votes and concurrence by*
" *promiſes of Reward and Preferment (which is the*
" *moſt diſhonourable and unthrifty Brokery that can be*
" *practiced in a Parliament,* which from this time
" was much practiced, and *brought many ill things*
" *to paſs)* than to prevail upon thoſe weighty
" and important arguments which would bear the
" light. Which *low artifice* raiſed the inſolence of
" thoſe, which would, *as eaſily as it had been,* have
" been ſtill over-ruled and ſuppreſſed ; and was
" quickly *diſcerned by thoſe others, who, upon the*
" *Principles of Honour and Wiſdom, had hitherto ſwayed*
" *the Houſe in all matters of public concernment,* and
" who now concluded, by thoſe new condeſcenſions,
" that the former ſober ſpirit and reſolution was
" laid aſide, and that peeviſh men would be com-
" pounded with ; and ſo reſolved to ſit ſtill, or look
" on, till the ſuccefs of the ſtratagem might be diſ-
" cerned." (*The Life of Edw. Earl of* CLARENDON ;
written by himſelf. v. 2. *p.* 285. *8vo.*)—How different this from your prolufions !

Of the inducement to adopt your " *expedient*," but too " *fucceſsful*," BOLINGBROKE alſo gives an account diſagreeing *tcto cœlo* from yours, and corroborative of what I have with no ſmall ſatisfaction juſt extracted. His ſentiments are too full to the purpoſe not to be offered to your peruſal. " This *expedient* of corrupting " Parliaments (ſays the noble author) began under " the adminiſtration of that boiſterous, over-bear- " ing, dangerous Miniſter, CLIFFORD. *As long as* " *there remained any pretence to ſay that the Court* " *was in the intereſt of the People, the expedient of* " *Bribery was neither wanted, nor practiced.* When " the Court was evidently in another intereſt, the " neceſſity and the practice of bribing the Repreſen- " tatives of the People commenced." *Works. v.* 2. *p.* 57. *4to.*

Conciſe as is this expoſition of the motives for having recourſe to Influence, little need be added except our increaſed experience of its truth, and that its ſphere of action has of late years been con- ſiderably enlarged. For ſince the publication of the Diſſertation on Parties, regal and miniſterial Influ- ence has, with diſaſtrous ſucceſs, ſtricken its roots wider and deeper. Its ramifications are ſhot out into every corner of the kingdom. Not to multiply autho- rities, [App. S.] I ſhall bring only one more ; and I bring Mr. BURKE to teſtify, that events for nearly a century and a half, fatally confirm all that the wiſdom of CLARENDON deprecated. On ſubmitting to the Houſe of Commons in 1780, his ſalutary " plan for " the better ſecurity of the Independency of Par- " liament,"

" liament," this Orator, with the eloquence of
truth, breaks out in this ſtrain—" What, I confeſs,
" was uppermoſt with me, what I bent the whole force
" of my mind to, was *the reduction of that corrupt In-*
" *fluence;* which is itſelf the perennial ſpring of all
" prodigality, and of all diſorder; which loads us
" more than millions of debt; which takes away
" vigour from our arms, wiſdom from our councils,
" and *every ſhadow of authority and credit from the*
" *moſt venerable parts of our Conſtitution."* (*Works.*
v. 2. *p.* 177.)—To theſe inconteſtible and unequivocal teſtimonies againſt you, I add no obſervation
of my own. I only pray judgement between us.———

As we are on the topic of " *terror,"* it is material
moreover to tell you, that at the ſame time that " *the*
" *King carried his meaſures in Parliament by intimida-*
" *tion;"* Judges at the devotion of the Court were
placed on the Bench to brow beat, and fine, and
impriſon Jurors who acquitted men obnoxious to
" *Government,"* if I may uſe the word in your con-
fined acceptation. Since BUSHELL's Caſe, * this
outrage has not been attempted; and, moſt happily for
our Lives and Liberties, Juries have hitherto eſcaped
the contamination of Influence. Diveſted of all Influence, their Verdicts of Not Guilty maintain a free
Preſs, and will ever (I hope) prove an inſuperable
bar to the cumulative, conſtructive Treaſons of
Crown-Lawyers. Had it happened otherwiſe, had
they not been left without hope and without fear, to
follow the dictates of their conſciences, ſhould we

---

* Vaughan's Rep. 135.

not

not have had a cautionary chapter from you to in-
culcate the necessity of the Influence of the Crown
on Juries? What a field to expatiate, that Jurymen,
if left to think and act for themselves, would never
convict seditious Libellers and Traitors. How
plausible that there should be the same "*expedient*"
to gain over Jurymen, as to gain over the Houses of
Parliament. For did not experience evince the contrary, it would have been *as* colourable a presump-
tion that without "*intimidation or Influence,*" Juries
would not discharge their duty to the country, as
that men freely and fairly chosen, would perversely
retard or reject in Parliament measures tending to
the benefit of the State.

It is futile to press on our recollection for the
purpose you would serve, the unhappy occurrences
occasioned by the contest between CHARLES the
first and the Parliament. I peremptorily deny that
his misfortunes can be justly referred to a want of
this sort of Influence. History vouches to the truth
of my assertion. Peruse the eventful period from
the compulsory abdication of JAMES, to the elevation of the House of Brunswic-Lunenburgh—when
Parliaments had nothing to dread, and little to expect, from the agents of the executive Government,
and when the effervescence necessarily attendant on
a Revolution, was far from subsided—when withal
numbers of the Commonwealth's men were yet alive
who must have cherished a fond remembrance of
" the good old cause." Lest I should trespass beyond the due bounds of epistolary diffusion, I select

proofs

proofs only during the reign of WILLIAM. He who, devoid of all prior claim, had the diadem fixed on his brow, upon certain terms and conditions by the gift of the People—He who had not Influence in Parliament fufficient to carry through his private and perfonal meafures—He who was *ten* years in procuring a Civil-Lift to be fettled on him for life— He who was compelled to revoke a grant to his Dutch favourite BENTINCK, and to fend away a Regiment of foreign Life-guards, " the companions " of his victories," whom he more than once importuned the Commons to fuffer him to keep about his perfon—He who was not always foothed with Addreffes echoing back the royal Speech, but who fometimes was mortified by fullen expoftulation, not to fay rude remonftrance—[App. T.]. He, Sir, even WILLIAM, fate fecurely. The memory of thefe things entitles me flatly to contradict your fuppofition. Further; it will be no eafy tafk for you to faften on a ftraggling incident of national detriment during this arduous reign, arifing either from Triennial Parliaments, or the non-exiftence of Influence. The good fenfe of the Nation, affured that its Liberties, civil and religious, depended on his wearing the Crown, and were fafe in his hand, fupported him againft the exiled hereditary Sovereign, formidable both by foreign alliance, and by numerous adherents within this Ifland.

Since WILLIAM, a foreigner, and of cold and repulfive demeanour, againft whom the minds of multitudes were inflamed by religious perfuafions, or

exafperated

exafperated by political prejudices, could by an elective title wield his fceptre fecurely and fuccefsfully, before the Influence of the Crown had obtained, and while Parliaments were no more than Triennial, and that without the fhadow of a perfonal claim—furely, Mr. PALEY, you infult the beft of Kings by fending abroad an idea that Influence is *now* necef-fary.—For a native prince adorned with attractions of private character that might be dangerous to the national Freedom, were they not counter-balanced by the goodnefs of his heart! What has he to fear? He fills the throne of his anceftors, and has feen his Court through a long reign thronged with the hereditary enemies of his Houfe, of a fudden tranf-formed into clofeft friends?—Let us be told no more of your hard option between a " *Government* " *by force*" and a " *Government of Influence*;" and may we apply with emulation and ardour to procure a Parliament as free from " *terror*," as fuperior to venality.

You next remark that " in the Britifh Colonies " of North America, the late Affemblies poffeffed " much of the power and conftitution of our Houfe " of Commons. *The King and Government of Great* " *Britain held no patronage in the country*, which " could create attachment and Influence fufficient " to counteract that reftlefs arrogating fpirit which " in popular affemblies, when left to itfelf, will " never brook an authority that checks and inter-' " feres with its own. To this caufe, excited per-
" haps

" haps by *some unseasonable provocations*, we may at-
" tribute, as to their true and proper original, we
" will not say *the misfortunes, but the changes* that
" have taken place in the British Empire."—p.
493. With much art you have kept out of sight
the great efficient cause of the secession of our
Transf-Atlantic brethren. What you glide over with
the smooth phrase of " *unseasonable provocations*" I
must push forward into notice.—The Anglo-Americans read their lesson in the fundamental principle
of English Liberties. Every argument against the
the right of CHARLES to levy Ship-money by pretence of Prerogative convinced them that they
ought to rank the disposal of their own Property by
legislative Trustees of their own appointment fore-
most among the prerogatives of freemen. By every
constitutional document, from the Statute of Talliage to the Speeches of CAMDEN against American
Taxation, [App. U.] they were instructed that to give
up the power of taxing themselves was to surrender
their dearest rights and most precious interests at dis-
cretion. True to their duty to themselves, after the
British Parliament declared its right " to bind them
" in all cases whatsoever," and when our House of
Commons by undertaking to give and grant their
money without their consent, actually assumed the
entire command of their fortunes, the English blood
boiled in their veins. Taxation without Representation *is* Tyranny, and your Parliament must belie
(remonstrated three millions of HAMDENS) those
principles of Freedom our common ancestors died

to

to maintain, before " it can take and ufe our pro-
" perty when and in what manner it pleafes *."
Perceiving that this country turned a deaf ear to
their appeal, they refufed to deliver themfelves up
to be the victims of STATUTEABLE PLUNDER †, and
renounced all dependence on us. After their refift-
ance had manifefted our inability to reduce them to
" unconditional fubmiffion" by the point of the ba-
yonet, conciliatory propofitions were tranfmitted to
the United States by fpecial Commiffioners fent to
them to concede, among other things, " that an agent
" or agents from the different States fhould have
" *the privilege of a Seat and a voice in the Parlia-*
" *ment of Great Britain ‡.*" But the feafon of re-
union had been contemned by the infolence or the
treachery of the then Miniftry, and every overture of
accommodation was rejected. *Procul abfit omen.*
May no fuch obdurate fatuity prefide in our councils when the hour arrives (it may be at hand) that
the Public at large, ftimulated by our growing burthens, at laft fet themfelves to a ferious inquiry—
whether it will not be more expedient to put themfelves and their property under the fafeguard of an

* See the *Addrefs in* 1774 *to the People of Great Britain from
the general Congrefs.*

† " Thefe devoted Colonies were judged to be in fuch a
" ftate, as to prefent victories without bloodfhed, and all the
" eafy emoluments of *ftatuteable plunder.*"—*Declaration of the
Congrefs, July,* 1775.

‡ See *the Britifh Commiffioners' Letter to the Congrefs in*
1778.

Integral Reprefentation than to leave their interefts
with an Affembly of which the major number is
appointed by a trifling and fictitious fraction of the
Nation? Whenever the mafs of the People beftow on this queftion the attention it deferves, they
will affuredly find that *Conftitutional Reform* is the effential preliminary to *Public Oeconomy*, not to infift
on other confiderations. Then they will reclaim
their exclufive right to the appointment of the Parliamentary Affeffors of the public Taxes. I turn
my eyes from the iffue of a refufal to reinftate them
in this rightful inheritance, after they have once
afked how can Taxmafters like the Cornifh Burgeffes, or the Delegates of the Scottifh Burghs, or
the Cinque-Port Barons, our *virtual* Reprefentors,
accord with that firft of conftitutional principles that
Englifhmen are to be taxed only by themfelves or
their Reprefentatives?

You, Sir, avoid this difcuffion, and affign a caufe
unfounded in fact for the defection of the Republic
of America. The Crown " *held*" very confiderable
" *patronage*" there. Almoft every place of power
and profit, from the Governor downward, in nearly
all the Colonies was in the difpofal of the Britifh
Court. In BOSTON even the Magiftrates were not
chofen by the inhabitants. But the dominion of
ftrangers is ever odious. When did a People abide
any length of time patient of deputed authority * ?

---

* The word *Rebellion (re-bellium)* befpeaks the propenfion of
a conquered People to revolt.

I do

I do not believe you will be able to point out a fingle inftance, where a Nation, when it felt itfelf fufficiently ftrong, delayed to fhake off Government
at *fecond-hand*.   Men are " *reftlefs*" under and ill
" *brook*" provincial dependency.   Witnefs a Sifter-
Ifland, governed on the exact model of our own,
though diftracted by religious diffenfions, and though
Influence has too much fway—Did not IRELAND
feize with ardour the " golden opportunity" to
emancipate herfelf from Englifh Legiflation ?—The
confequences of this unhappy ftruggle lie heavy on
us, and long muft they lie.   They are a fine we muft
be content to pay for *our* folly or crime.   If it were
time to feparate, why did we not part on friendly
terms ?   Then the remembrance of paft kindneffes,
and the interchange of benevolent offices, endearing
us to each other, muft have conftantly ftrengthened
the mutual ties of intereft and blood.   Perhaps the
Anglo-Americans were children arrived at ma-
turity, who ftood no longer in need of the tutelage
of the mother-country. Becaufe the parent-ftate af-
fifted in regulating and protecting the infant-efta-
blifhments of her offspring, could the right foliow
to coerce them in their riper years till " proftrate
" at her feet ?"—It was by infolence in her rulers
like this, and not through any want of Influence,
that BRITAIN precipitated the lofs of, if fhe did not
throw away, her American territories. By me-
naces like thefe, and by conduct equally infatuated,
we fucceeded in alienating their minds, and at laft

drove

drove the irritated Colonists to exclaim with one heart and one voice,

"" Fas mihi Graiorum facrata refolvere jura,

"" Fas odiffe viros ;··

"" ····················· ··········· teneor patriæ nec legibus ullis.""

LET-

LETTER IV.

" No flavery can be fo effectually brought and fixed upon us
" as *Parliamentary flavery. By the Corruption of Parliament, and*
" *the abfolute* INFLUENCE *of a King, or his Minifter, on the*
" *two Houfes,* we return into that ftate, to deliver or fecure us
" from which Parliaments were inftituted, and are really go-
" vern.d by the arbitrary will of one man. Our whole Confti-
" tution is at once diffolved. *Many fecurities to Liberty are pro-*
" *vided, but the integrity which depends on the Freedom and In-*
" *dependency of Parliament, is the key-ftone that keeps the whole to-*
" *gether.* If this be fhaken our Conftitution totters. If it be
" quite removed cur Conftitution falls into ruin.—The fingle.
" reign of HENRY the eighth will ferve to fhow, that *no ty-*
" *ranny can be more fevere than that which is exercifed by a con-*
" *cert with Parliament* ; that arbitrary Will may be made the
" fole rule of Government, even *while the names and forms of*
" *a free Conftitution are preferved ;* that for a Prince, or his Mi-
" nifter, to become our tyrant, there is no need to abolifh
" Parliaments ; there is no need that he who is mafter of one
" part of the Legiflature fhould endeavour to abolifh the other
" two, when he can ufe upon every occafion the united ftrength
" of the whole ; there is no need he fhould be a tyrant in the
" grofs, when he can be fo in detail, nor in name, when he
" can be fo in effect ; that for Parliaments to eftablifh tyran-
" ny, there is no need therefore to repeal Magna Charta, or
" any other of the great fupports of our Liberty. *It is enough,*
" *if they put themfelves corruptly and fervilely under the* INFLUENCE
" *of fuch a Prince, or fuch a Minifter.*—On the whole, I con-
" clude that in the poffible cafe here fuppofed, the firft and
" principal object will be *to deftroy the Conftitution, under pretence*
" *of preferving the Government, by corrupting our Parliaments.*—
" There is furely too much reafon to fufpect that *the enemies of*
" *our Conftitution* may attempt hereafter to govern by Corrup-
" tion *when it is pleaded for and recommended, as a neceffary ex-*
                                                        " *pedient*

" *pedient of Government, by men whose birth, education, and for-*
" *tune, aggravate their crime and their folly; by men whom Honor,*
" *at leaſt, ſhould reſtrain from favoring ſo diſhonorable a cauſe;*
" *and* BY MEN WHOSE PECULIAR OBLIGATIONS TO PREACH
" UP MORALITY *ſhould reſtrain them at leaſt from being the*
" PREACHERS OF AN IMMORALILY, ABOVE ALL OTHERS,
" ABOMINABLE IN ITS NATURE, AND PERNICIOUS IN
" ITS EFFECTS."——BOLINGBROKE; *Works, v.* 2. *p.* 137.
4to.

SIR,

As I borrowed the motto to my laſt Letter from
LOCKE, I have prefixed one to the preſent from
BOLINGBROKE, to ſhow you that the moſt eminent
of the Whigs and the Tories, men who perhaps
accord on no other point, unite in their deteſtation
of that Influence on Parliament, to which you are
ſo devoutly attached.—Muſt it not aſtoniſh every
one that you, in the chair of Morality, promulgate
doctrines which revolt even the moral feelings of a
BOLINGBROKE?

Were it not for the pernicious conſequences, it
would be amuſive to contemplate how imperceptibly
and plauſibly mankind are beguiled by the power
of words. Till of late years, money was taken
from us by the plain old word a *Tax*; now as the
Language refines, our purſes are emptied by a *Com-
mutation.* In like manner, practices, when branded
as Bribery and Corruption, ſtartled our anceſtors:
but ſince this coarſe phraſeology has paſſed away
with the faſhion of the times, the things themſelves
ſeem, by the magic of ſounds, to have caſt off
their

their offensive properties, and to you and to others, appear not harmless merely, but highly useful under the more polished shape of Influence.

"*When the mind is once taught to endure without* " *uneasiness a consciousness of guilt the character is pre-* " *pared for every compliance.*" There you breathe the genuine spirit of Morality. The moral sense is soon worn callous. The first theme therefore, and the last with writers who have instructed mankind in their "duty toward their neighbours," has been the *inviolability of Principle.* They draw a strait and perspicuous line between right and wrong. Not so the apologist for Pension-Parliaments. The nature of that subject necessitated you to soften down its harshness of feature; but the shades of difference are so dubious that, to common perceptions, the tints melt into each other. Reflections, such as these, occurred to me on reading your " protest against any " construction by which what is here said shall be " attempted to be applied to the justification of " bribery, or of any clandestine reward or solicita- " tion whatever. The very *secrecy* of such nego- " ciations *confesses* or begets a consciousness of guilt, " —Our *apology* relates solely to that Influence, " which results from the acceptance or expectation " of public preferments."—p. 494. In turning over the leaves of your production we perpetually recal the sentiments of former writers, frequently copied literally, and always without acknowlege-ment. [App. W.] Yet in the striking resemblance I have now to point out there is no suspicion of

pla-

plagiarifm. Similarity of fituation naturally fuggefted the fimilarity of the diftinction. *Father Foigard* is quieting the fcruples of a Lady's Maid, whom he tempted by the offer of a few guineas to betray her Miftrefs. " Won't the money look like a *bribe,* " Doctor"—afks the Waiting Woman ? The reverend Cafuift fatisfies her by replying with all becoming gravity—" if you receive the money be- " forehand 'twill be, *logicé a bribe;* but if you ftay " till afterward, 'twill be *only a gratification* !"— Wonderfully does the Jefuit-Confeffor chime in unifon with the Moralift. You, Sir, intreat us to believe your political cafuiftry is not to reconcile " *bribery*" to tender confciences. Heaven forbid ! Your " *apology relates folely to the Influence arifing* " *from the acceptance or expectation of public prefer-* " *ments !*"

Serioufly, your " *proteft againft Bribery,*" Mr. PALEY, comes very aukwardly, knowing as you muft that *your* Houfe of Commons, with only HALF of its Members chofen legally and conftitutionally, can never be filled without it. In my eyes, he who receives a fum at once appears lefs dangerous than he whofe continuance in a poft of profit depends on his Vote. Of a Penfion, as well as of a Sinecure, there can be but one opinion ; and what is a Place with a Salary but a ftanding " *bribe ?*" And therefore a Claufe, now repealed, was inferted in the Act of Settlement, to incapacitate any falaried or penfioned

---

* See the *Beaux Stratagem,* by *Farquahar.*

perfon

person from serving as a Member of the House of Commons. An advantageous appointment for a Member or his relative may be a more decent vehicle to convey a reward for Parliamentary services; but when a poison is in some degree disguised, the greater is the danger.—You favour permanent " *bribery*" by lucrative " *preferments,*" but forbid the occasional acceptance of sums of money: as consistently might you plead for Felony and prohibit petit Larceny. In your mode of reasoning, the Journeyman Weaver, whose " poverty but not his " will consents," to take a " *bribe*" for his Suffrage, to contribute toward the subsistance of a starving family, is more criminal than the worthless Member, who commanding all the necessaries and comforts of life, vilely hires out his voice for the emoluments of office, and turns a traitor to the People that he may riot in luxury and extravagance.

You now observe that " in political above all " other subjects, the arguments, or rather the con- " jectures on each side of a question, are often so " equally poized, that the wisest judgements may " be held in suspence. These I call subjects of " *indifference.* But again, when the subject is not " *indifferent* in itself, it will appear such to *a great* " *part* of those to whom it is proposed, for want of " information, or reflection, or experience, or ca- " pacity, to collect and weigh the reasons by which " either side is supported. These are subjects of " *apparent indifference.*"—p. 494. Finding myself utterly unable to guess what you intend by " *political* " *subjects*

" *fubjects of indifference*," I greatly regret that inftead of this gratuitous affumption, you did not
ftoop to exemplify your hypothefis by facts * How
can we encounter phantoms? For one, I am yet
to learn what folitary Vote of a public nature can
be called " *indifferent.*" Was any Vote, for example, which would have helped to preferve PEACE
and PLENTY " *indifferent* ?" Is any Vote either really
or " *apparently indifferent*" which would help to ftop
the wide-fpread miferies of WAR, after fad experience had fhown that the attainment of the object
propofed was as impracticable as it was deteftable,
and that to perfevere was only to accumulate expence
and difgrace? Or, is any Vote " *indifferent*" which
extends the revenue-code of pains and penalties to
invade the fecurity of domeftic life, no longer per-
mitting the trader under the dominion of the Ex-
cise to be the mafter of his door?—What *is* the
regulation of interior œconomy, or what the queftion
of foreign policy, that five hundred and fifty-eight
chofen Englifhmen are incompetent to decide? To
qualify for attendance on public bufinefs requires no
fuperlative powers of intellect, as you feem to think.
The means to form a found opinion on public tranf-
actions are acceffible to the underftandings of plain
men. Recent experience is fpreading the perfuafion

* " He that would not deceive himfelf, ought to build his
" hypothefis on matter of fact, and make it out by fenfible
" experience, and not prefume on matter of fact becaufe of
" his hypothefis, that is becaufe he fuppofes it to be fo."—
LOCKE; *Effay on Human Underftanding. b.* 2. *ch.* 1. *f.* 10.

wider and wider that the luminous endowments of our Statesmen have tended rather to dazzle and to mislead by their illusive brilliancy than to elucidate right courses for national prosperity. Whether you are to be numbered among those who do not discriminate between the gift of oratory and the faculty of judgement I know not, I am one who have long thought the blaze of eloquence is oftener employed to fascinate or inflame than to illuminate. To me it appears that the light of common sense shining in well-intentioned and uninfluenced breasts would be a sufficient, probably the safest, guide to an Assembly of Legislators *.—I repeat my request that you would give some examples of these myste-

---

* After SWIFT has with his peculiar plainness enforced and illustrated the competency of popular Assemblies, I should be without excuse, were I to dwell longer on that point. " Let " us suppose (says this writer) five hundred men, mixed in " point of sense and honesty, as usually assemblies are; and let " us suppose these men proposing, debating, resolving, voting " according to the mere natural motions of their own little or " much reason and understanding; I do allow, that abundance " of indigested and abortive, many pernicious and foolish over- " tures would arise and float a few minutes, but then they " would die and disappear. Because this must be said in be- " half of human kind, that common sense and plain reason " while men are disengaged from acquired opinions, will ever " have some general influence upon their minds; whereas the " species of folly and vice are infinite, and so different in " every individual, that they could never procure a majority, " if other corruptions did not enter to pervert men's understandings, " and misguide their wills."—Of the Contests and Dissentions in " Athens and Rome. ch. 5.

ries

ries in the occult fcience of Government—thefe Parliamentary enigmas, which would appear inexplicable to " *a great part of* " an Affembly that in your eftimation is compofed " *of the moft confider-* " *able Landholders and Merchants of the Kingdom ;* " *the heads of the Army, the Navy, and the Law,* " *the occupiers of the great Offices in the State ; to-* " *gether with many private individuals eminent by their* " *knowlege, eloquence, or activity.*"—Are thefe your accomplifhed Legiflators, whom you now think it convenient to degrade as " *wanting information, or* " *reflection, or experience, or capacity to collect and* " *weigh the reafons by which either fide is fupported?*" You are entangled in your own web beyond the poffibility of extrication. When diffuading us from a Reform in the Reprefentation, you fcruple not to afk, " *does any new fcheme promife to collect together* " MORE WISDOM *or produce firmer integrity?*"— Your arguments are at crofs purpofes. Now, offering excufes for our Election-fyftem, you think fit to aver that " *in the feveral plans which have been fug-* " *gefted of an equal or a reformed Reprefentation, it* " *will be difficult to difcover any propofal that has a* " *tendency to throw more of the bufinefs of the Nation* " *into the Houfe of Commons, or to collect* A SET OF " MEN MORE FIT TO TRANSACT THAT BUSINESS, " *or in general more interefted in the national happi-* " *nefs and profperity.*"—*p.* 490. Now, apologizing for the Influence of the Crown, with ludicrous inconfiftency you affirm that " *to a great part*" of this very beft of all poffible collections ot the

G   " *wifdom*

" *wisdom and integrity*" of the whole British Nation,
the most important questions appear " *indifferent*"—
Nay, that " *for want of information, or reflection, or*
" *experience, or capacity,*" they are incapable of
" *weighing the reasons by which either side is supported.*"
But the " *acceptance or expectation of public prefer-*
" *ments*" makes every thing " plain and clear" to
the meanest understandings *. *Ibi fas, ubi max-
ima merces.* On every Division they who " *want*
" *capacity*" to discern the public interest can obey the
beck of the Minister.

You afterward allege, " according as the dif-
" position of Parliament is friendly or adverse to
" the *recommendation* of the Crown in matters which
" are *really* or *apparently indifferent,* as *indifference*
" hath been now explained, the business of empire
" will be transacted *with ease and conveniency,* or em-
" barrassed with endless contention and difficulties."
p. 495. Again I have to express my regret that
you should have rested content with vague alle-
gations. Assertions might be answered by assertions.
But I call on you, Sir, to specify *when* the business of

* However your argument may create surprise, it is yours
only by adoption.

" *What makes all doctrines plain and clear?*
" *About two hundred pounds a year.*
" *And that which was prov'd true before,*
" *Prove false again?—Two hundred more.*"
Hudibras, part 3. *cant.* 1. *v.* 1277.

The praise indeed of using it gravely belongs wholly to
yourself.

the

the Britifh empire was fo " *embarraffed with conten-* " *tion and difficulties*" in Parliament before the pre- valence of Influence as to be prejudicial to the Nation ? And what meafure of national good, fince its introduction among us, it is probable would have mifcarried, had not this Influence been applied ? Yet any one unacquainted with the hiftory of Parlia- mentary proceedings, muft imagine, from the gloomy picture which you paint of " *embarraffments,* " *endlefs contentions and difficulties*" that an inde- pendent Parliament had proved one of the fevereft vifitations of Providence. We fhould fearch in vain to find paffages of Armies loft, of Commerce haraffed, of Cultivation blafted, and of Famine occafioned, or of the Empire difmembered, by the " *adverfe dif-* " *pofition of Parliament to the recommendation of the* " *Crown.*" At this ftage, verging toward a con- clufion, I ftay not to enquire whether Armies have been loft, Commerce has been haraffed, the Empire difmembered, or Famine occafioned, by the facile ductility of temper, characteriftic of modern Par- liaments.

I was apt to believe that the more ftrictly the legiflative, executive, and judiciary offices were kept apart, the better were their refpective faculties ad- miniftered. The laft exercife of the royal Negative was, I believe, on a Place-bill. Your fears contain the firft excufe I have feen for WILLIAM's un- gracious refufal of his affent ; and till I met with your work, I was unapprized of the debt of gratitude due to our Upper Houfe for their regular rejection

of

of the Place-bills fince fent to them by the Commons. Had thefe Bills paffed into laws, they muft
have checked the accumulation of jarring functions
and difcordant powers on one head. But then we
could not have prevented this confufion of public
authorities without the *hazard* of rendering Parliaments independent!—A Reprefentor of the People,
too anxious for their welfare to fubfcribe his belief
in the monftrous doctrine ftarted by influenced Parliaments, the doctrine of CONFIDENCE in Minifters,
and inheriting that honourable jealoufy of the executive Government to which we owe every thing
that is dear, will entertain a more enlarged opinion
of the obligations of his truft. He will not feel your
folicitude for the " *eafe and conveniency*" of public officers, when fet in competition with that vigilant cir-
cumfpection he knows it to be his bounden duty to
exert. Habituated to fevere attention, and ftrenuous
in remonftrance where the occafion requires, there
will not, I fay, Sir, in a well-informed and faithful
Reprefentative exift your tender intereft for " *the*
" *eafe and conveniency*" of the ftipendiary admini-
ftrators of the executive Government. Every other
confideration will with him be fubordinate to the
falus Reipublicæ. He will require his confcience to be
informed before he can ratify any minifterial meafure
by his vote. He will remember and apply to your
remark, what the celebrated Commentator on our
Laws has left on record, left infractions of the TRIAL
BY JURY fhould ever pafs unheeded—" That the
" Liberties

" Liberties of England cannot but fubfift fo long as
" this Palladium remains facred and inviolate; not
" only from all open attacks, which none will be fo
" hardy as to make, but alfo from all fecret ma-
" chinations which may fap and undermine it; and
" however *convenient* thefe may appear at firft, as
" doubtlefs ALL ARBITRARY POWERS WELL-EXE-
" CUTED ARE THE MOST CONVENIENT, yet let it
" again be remembered that *delays and little incon-*
" *veniencies are the price that all free Nations muft pay*
" *for their Liberty in more fubftantial matters*, and that
" thefe inroads upon the facred bulwark of the
" Nation are fundamentally oppofite to the fpirit of
" our Conftitution." BLACKSTONE; *b.* 4. *ch.* 27.—
Under defpotic Governments we well know " *the*
" *eafe and conveniency*" of thofe in power outweighs
all regard to public utility. But the Englifh Nation
will, I truft, ever affert their Government to have
been inftituted for the People's fake, and that therefore *their* collective " *eafe and conveniency*," not that
of Minifters, ought to be the fole rule and fixed
principle of their Reprefentors *.—I do not fufpect

you

---

* BOLINGBROKE has anticipated and fet afide your plea of
" *conveniency*" fo happily that I cannot refrain from another
quotation. " Muft all the forms (he afks) inftituted to preferve
" the checks and controls of the feveral parts of the Conftitution
" on one another, *and neceffary by confequence to preferve the liberty*
" *of the whole*, be abandoned, and a free Conftitution be de-
" ftroyed, for the fake of fome little *conveniency*, or expe-
" diency the more, *in the administration of public affairs ?* &c.—In
" fhort, we muft make our option, and furely this option is not

" hard

you to prefer the flavifh acquiefcence and profound myftery of a Turkifh Divan to the Freedom of *Speech*, and the open Debates of an Englifh Parliament. You only mifconceive the animation of the loud language of Liberty :

" What tho' among ourfelves with too much heat
" We fometimes wrangle, when we fhould debate ;
" A confequential ill which Freedom draws ;
" A bad effect, but from a noble caufe."——

" Nor is it (you continue) a conclufion *founded*
" *in juftice or experience !* that, becaufe men are in-
" duced by views of intereft to yield their confent
" or fupport to meafures, concerning which their
" judgment decides nothing, they may be brought
" by the fame Influence to act in deliberate op-
" pofition to knowlege and duty." p. 495.
The Influence you advocate is not an " *Influence*
" *which will bring men to act in deliberate oppofition to*
" *knowlege and duty*" ! You muft then have forgotten, or hoped that your readers would forget, that " *fure and commanding Influence of which the Con-*
" *ftitution, it feems, is totally ignorant, growing out of*
" *that enormous patronage, which the increafed extent*

" hard to be made, between the real and permanent bleffings
" of Liberty, diffufed thro' a whole nation, and the fantaftic
" and accidental advantages, *which they who govern*, not the
" body of the People, enjoy under abfolute Monarchies."

Differt. on Parties. Let. 11.

" *and*

" *and opulence of the empire has placed in the difposal of*
" *the Executive Magiftrate.*" p. 466.

In good faith, *do* you fuppofe that thofe would not
" *act in deliberate oppofition to knowlege and duty,*" whom
you efteem dead to all the compunctions of fhame—
as fo little regarding the national welfare, that, if not
influenced by " *views of intereft,*" they would " *at*
" *leaft obftruct the conduct of public affairs by a wanton*
" *and perverfe oppofition ?*" As if men fo abandoned
as to make a merchandize of their Parliamentary
truft could be ftruck with remorfe, and fhrink from
any project they were ordered to fupport. No, Sir,
Put no man's intereft in the balance againft his duty,
is the deduction from " *experience.*" In a ftruggle
between duty and felf-intereft, it is not uncharitable
to apprehend that the latter will triumph. When
BACON profeffed *not to fell injuftice, but never to let*
Juftice go fcotfree, he compromifed with his duty
under the femblance of a pliant Morality, precifely
the fame as you here tolerate—he would not for
lucre do that which was wrong in the exercife of his
judiciary functions, nor what was right without that
fort of " *Influence which refults from the acceptance or*
" *expectation*" of perfonal recompence. No doubt
too he flattered himfelf he could never be " *brought*
" *to act in deliberate oppofition to knowlege and duty.*"
He remains a perpetual warning that if we ca-
pitulate with intereft by a natural progreffion it
is fure to overpower the ftrongeft refolutions.—
" The wifeft of mankind" defcended from the

G 4　　　　　　　Judgment

Judgment-Seat with ignominy, convicted of foul corruption *.

It is certainly unsafe, perhaps it is unjust, to place any one between temptation on the one hand, and moral obligation on the other. In the summary ordinances of Moses to the " Judges and Officers" of the Israelites, his most pointed injunction is against their " taking a gift." Directly contrary to your opinion, " a gift (says the inspired Law-giver) doth " blind the eyes of the wife, and pervert the words " of the righteous." (*Exodus. ch.* 28. *v.* 8. and *Deut. ch.* 16. *v.* 19.) Perhaps it is scarcely decorous to remind you that this restraint was laid on rulers elected by the People, and under a Theocracy.

In your general principle, that the *private vice* of a Legislator acting on the sordid motive of pecuniary interest is a *public benefit*, you vie with MANDEVILLE; and, like MANDEVILLE, you would qualify your system by setting bounds to the practice. [App. X.] But, to recur to the melancholy " *experience*" of the age in which we live in opposition to the chimerical refinements, and idle distinctions you attempt. Mark how plainly Mr. DUNNING (Lord ASHBURTON) puts you down. Hearken to this powerful speaker and constitutional Lawyer, where he says, that " nothing less than the most alarming and " corrupt *Influence, could induce a number of Gentlemen*

* Της δι Δικης ροδος ιλκομενης τ κ'ανδρες αγωσι
ΔΩΡΟΦΑΓΟΙ, σκολιαις δι δικαις κρινωσι Θεμιστας.

ΗΣΙΟΔΟΥ Εργαι και Ημεραι.

" *in*

" *in that Houfe, to fupport the Minifter by their Votes*
" *in thofe meafures within doors,* WHICH THEY CON-
" DEMNED AND REPROBATED WITHOUT. *That this*
" *was the cafe, and within his own immediate knowlege,*
" *he declared upon his honour* ; and added, that tho'
" he was not himfelf very fqueamifh, nor over-
" delicate, in giving his opinion upon the meafures
" of Adminiftration, *he had never indulged himfelf in*
" *throwing upon them fuch fevere epithets, as had fallen*
" *in his prefence from the mouths of Members abroad,*
" *who notwithftanding* SUPPORTED THEM WITHIN
" THESE WALLS!! Nor was the number fmall, for,
" but that the tafk would be too invidious, *he could*
" *mention no lefs than* FIFTY *Members of that Houfe who*
" *had held that language and conduct.*"—See *Parlia-*
mentary Debates, April 6, 1780.

They who are not ftricken dumb by this aftevera-
tion of the numbers within one man's knowlege " who
" dare think one thing, and another *vote*," * have to
folve a vexatious problem. *How* in the fignal cafe
of the Middlefex Election, Mr. WILKES, four times
chofen, was as often expelled by the Houfe, who at
laft feated a Gentleman of *their* choice in the place

---

* " You would not expect to hear any *lax, fafhionable, tem-*
" *porizing principles of Morality* from the Pulpit. Alas! let us
" fpeak as plainly as we can, we have no great expectations of
" being regarded; it is the laft ftage of political profligacy
" *when men condemn in private, condemn in unequivocal terms, and*
" *without a blufh, the very principles which they fupport in public.*"

Sermons and Tracts, by R. WATSON, *Bifhop of Landaff. p.* 122.

of

of the Candidate elected by the Freeholders? Their task will not end here. The sticklers for " *the In-* " *fluence arising from the acceptance or expectation of* " *public preferments*," have further to develope, *how* the same and succeeding Houses, though pressed every Session to wipe away this blot from the Journals of Parliament, negatived all Motions with that purport, till Lord NORTH, who auspicated this expulsion had been displaced? Then the change of Ministry effected a sudden change in the minds of the House of Commons. To what latent cause are we to ascribe this revolution in their sentiments? Are we bound to suppose that by a blind and irresistible fatality these unnatural Majorities were robbed of free-agency, and degraded to involuntary instruments to execute what others had devised? Or may we ask, whether the secret workings of a corrupt ascendancy through " *the acceptance* " *and expectation of public preferments*" did not IN- FLUENCE them, and " *in deliberate opposition to know-* " *lege and duty*," to do a deed " subversive of the " rights of the whole body of Electors in the king- " dom?" * And to persist just so many years in their refusal to cancel this alarming precedent as that Ministerial Influence continued, which instigated the opprobrious Resolution?

* 3d May, 1782. "It was resolved that all the Declarations, " Orders, and Resolutions respecting the Election of John " Wilkes, Esq. for the County of Middlesex, as a void Elec- " tion, &c. be expunged from the Journals of this House *as* " *subversive of the rights of the whole body of Electors of the King-* " *dom.*"

At

At length we are arrived at your courtly corrollary, which by the perplexity and ambiguity of expreſſion we may collect, envelopes more meaning than is avowed. You admoniſh us to " reflect upon the
" power of the Houſe of Commons to extort a com-
" pliance with its reſolutions from the other parts
" of the Legiſlature, or to put to *death the Conſtitution*
" *by a refuſal of the annual grants of money* to the
" ſupport of the neceſſary functions of Government
" —when we reflect, alſo, what motives there
" are, which, in the viciſſitudes of political in-
" tereſts and paſſions, *may one day* arm and point
" this power againſt the Executive Magiſtrate—
" when we attend to theſe conſiderations, we ſhall
" be led *perhaps* to acknowlege, that *there is not*
" *more of paradox than of probability*, in that impor-
" tant, but much decriéd apothegm, *that an inde-*
" *pendent Parliament is incompatible with the exiſtence*
" *of the Monarchy."* p. 496. True it is, Sir, the Houſe of Commons have in theory the power to withhold " *the annual grants of money."* But this power now reſts merely *in ſcriptis.* Of what avail is a right which they may continue to claim, but can never exerciſe ? To this *artificial* reaſoning, not unlike the technical fictions which diſgrace the *letter* of our Law, it is enough for my preſent purpoſe to repeat that " the Supplies they muſt vote, for the
" Army muſt have its pay, and the Public Credi-
" tors their intereſt." [App. Y.] More might be ſaid to allay your fears on this ſcore, but I haſten to aſk you if this can be the ſelf-ſame body, which,

3   when

when it fuited, you defcribed as fallen into a ftate
fo abject and fo weak, that prudence forbade them
to fhake off the interference of the Peers in their Elections? They muft fubmit paffively to this abufe, " *to*
" *help to keep the Government of the country*" in their
hands; in which you were pleafed to add, " *it would not*
" *perhaps long continue to refide, if fo powerful and wealthy*
" *a part of the Nation as the Peerage compofe, were ex-*
" *cluded from all fhare and intereft in its conftitution.*"—
  That all may comprehend the more clearly its
general afpect, let me detain you while I fketch a
parting view of your performance.—Had you fpoken
out roundly, and declared that to intruft any powers
to the People's Houfe, other than to regulate an
inclofure-bill, or a road-act, were highly dangerous
to the common fafety, if not counter-acted by the
Influence of the Crown; however the doctrine
would have outraged our countrymen, at any rate
you might have lain claim to the merit of publifh-
ing fentiments of which you were not afhamed. But
to contend, that, to the neglect of a free choice, it is
better for " HALF *of the Houfe of Commons to obtain*
" *their Seats by purchafe or nomination*"—To affert
that if men with fpecious qualifications be returned,
" *it fignifies little who return them*"—To enquire
whether " *any new fcheme promife to collect more wifdom*
" *and integrity*"—To defend the Peers in their interference in the Election of the Commons—To
afk, " *where would be the inconveniency if the King*
" *fhould nominate a limited number*"—To have
doubted whether any endeavour to diminifh the Influence

fluence of the Crown " *be good or even* INNOCENT"—
To suppose the Commons atrocious enough, unless
gained by private and particular interest, " *to obstruct*
" *the conduct of public affairs by a wanton and perverse*
" *oppofition*"—To leave us only the choice between
a " *Government of terror,*" or a " *Government by In-*
" *fluence*"—To pronounce the national business so
complex that in general it is " *indifferent*" to Members on which side they vote—To declare, " *ex-*
" *perience*" teaches that interest will not make men
" *act in oppofition to knowlege and duty*"—To crown
the whole with an " *apothegm*" that " *an indepen-*
" *dent Parliament is incompatible with Monarchy.*"—
And to hold out this tiffue of libellous inuendoes on
the cardinal principles of the English Constitution,
not more our honest pride than the common topic
of praise among foreigners, in order to raise doubts
and difficulties concerning their excellency, and that
on no better ground than a remote and improbable
poffibility—This wild furmife, which at last you
can only venture to call a " *probability*" of what
" *may one day*" happen—that a fair and uninfluenced
Reprefentative of the Commons may " *put to death*
" *the Conftitution*"—is furely premeditated equivo-
cation—Yes, I muft call it difhonourable duplicity.
This tamenefs deceives our expectation. Why
faulter ? Obvioufly your context demands a bolder
climax.

I have an heavier charge againft you. Your
project to fence the Conftitution againft popular
excefs, by encircling the Throne with a regulated

conflux of Influence—that is, to open the flood-
gates of Corruption, hoping to shut them again
when the baleful tide flows to a given height in Parliament—is a libel on a Constitution compounded
like ours, of three INDEPENDENT Estates. " The
" integrity," according to Mr. PALEY, " which
" depends on the FREEDOM AND INDEPENDENCY OF
" PARLIAMENT, is the key-stone which keeps the
" whole together" no longer. Now Influence ce-
ments our social edifice. Touch this talisman, and
the baseless fabric dissolves. All the encomiums on
the happy assemblage of Monarchy, Aristocracy,
and Democracy, in the English scheme of Parliamentary Legislation are then no more than the waking
dreams of theorists ! Illuminated men throughout
Europe, the MONTESQUIEUS and the BURLAMAQUIS,
have in vain exhausted their talents to praise this
triple division and balance of powers, which, by a
free action of all its parts, gives reciprocal solidity
to each branch, while, by a rare felicity, it combines monarchical energy with the mild and equal
maxims of a Commonwealth. You forebode that a
free Parliament and the regal office could not co-
exist. Yet if " *the body of the British People be satis-*
" *fied with their condition*" (as you have more re-
cently told us *) how come you to fear that an
Assembly of *their* Delegates, voluntarily chosen to
speak *their* voice, and to defend *their* interests, would
prove " *incompatible with the existence of the Monarchy ?*"

---

* In the Advertisement to the separate publication of this
Chapter on the British Constitution.

whisper

Every whifper of this kind implies, neceffarily implies, one of thefe two things—either that Public Opinion is weary of kingly Government, or that the Crown and the Commons' Houfe are natural antagonifts. Extricate yourfelf out of this unfortunate dilemma. Let me add, without offence, that I fufpect this corollary to your political lucubrations would have been fpared, had it not been to work on our tried attachment to Royalty, in the hope to fright us from Conftitutional Reform. At leaft you muft wifh it to be fuppreffed after you are fhown its exprefs Parliamentary reprobation, even in the decay of modern Reprefentation. This was, Sir, during a tranfient fufpenfion of Influence, when the Houfe of Commons, recovering its proper tone, declared in an addrefs to the Throne, that " a King of Great " Britain cannot have fo perfect, [n] or fo honour- " able a fecurity for every thing which can make a " King truly great, and truly happy, as *in the* " *genuine and natural fupport of an* UNINFLUENCED " AND INDEPENDENT HOUSE OF COMMONS." *

Laftly : from your conjectural objections (they are nothing more) built on a " *probability*" of what " *may one day*" happen from an outrageous abufe of power by a popular Affembly, but in proof of which you are as unable to intimate a fingle indica-tion, as you are to exhibit a fatisfactory precedent, let us appeal to an infallible teft. To thefe fpecu-lative predictions I will oppofe plain matter of fact, the unvaried and collective evidence of different

* 15 Ap. 1782. Jour. Com. v. 38. p. 923.

ages,

ages, and of many countries. An accumulation of teftimony equivalent to demonftration : and, unlefs you were able to draw up a counter-catalogue, equally impreffive, every " unplaced, unpenfioned," *un-influenced* Englifhman, muft invert your fervile " *apothegm*" to affirm that A DEPENDENT PAR-LIAMENT IS INCOMPATIBLE WITH THE EXISTENCE OF A FREE CONSTITUTION. For, let the Englifh People weigh well in their minds that the Romans were deprived of Freedom by the abafement of the Senate—that the antient States General of France were reduced to a nullity by the fway which a tyrant gained over them—that the political profligacy of the Swedifh Diet deteriorated an elective and limited Monarchy into one hereditary and abfolute—that the Cortes of the various provinces of Spain com-pofed the moft independent and moft refpectable Affemblies that Europe had then feen, till the pre-cious ores of Peru and Mexico, tempted them to fubvert the Liberties of their country. Nor let us forget the fate of the States of Hungary and Bo-hemia ; nor that in the Electorates and other Co-Eftates of the Empire, fcarcely a veftige remains of their antient popular inftitutions—all are fuperfeded by a MILITARY DESPOTISM. Furthermore, let us bear uppermoft with our remembrance of thefe afflicting examples, that thefe Nations, humbled by flavery, loft their importance in the proportion that they loft their Freedom.

To pafs over the reft, Spain, heretofore the fcourge and terror of Europe, eminently bleffed by nature with the eternal advantages of fituation and climate, and annually fupplied with fterling treafure from the American Continent, has, fince that fatal reverfe, dwindled to an adverfary too feeble to crufh the corfairs of Barbary. What feries of calamity, arifing from the People enjoying their rights, have you to fet off againft this monitory recital of inflaved millions, where the legiflative Body corrupted by the executive Magiftrate, in alliance indeed in moft cafes with intriguing Priefts, has betrayed to a Tyrant the Liberties it was efpecially chofen to vindicate? The Prince grafps the folid fubftance of arbitrary power, and nothing is left to the Subject except the pageant of Freedom. I deny not that the " unreal mockery" of a Senate, a Parliament, a Diet, the Cortes, or the States, has been generally kept up, at leaft for a time, becaufe perverted into an inftrument truly formidable to the People. The prefervation of forms conceals the progreffion toward defpotifm. Defpotifm is a fpectre too hideous to gain admittance among free-born men, unlefs it be introduced under a borrowed mafk. Hiftory had evinced it to have been no mean policy in the Cæfars, long after their will was taken for the only law, to retain the external form and image of the Republic. *Eadem magiftratuum vocabula, fua confulibus, fua prætoribus fpecies.* It is not in *religious* eftablifhments only that " *the* NAME " *is commonly the laft thing that is changed.*" * Hence

---

* PALEY, p. 580.

it

it is, and the fact deserves our most serious regards, that the Sicilians, exhausted and gasping under Spanish oppression, are still insulted with the solemn grimace of the PARLIAMENT, founded by their Norman ancestors. [App. Z.] But we need not to look abroad in quest of instances. *They may be found at home.*—Your own Houses of Convocation, Sir, once the rivals of Parliament, are still, after the idle formality of Elections, to represent the Clergy, hung out on every General Election, to warn Englishmen how long the lifeless corse of an institution may remain entire after its spirit is departed.

APPEN.

Note A. referred to from p. 6.

*A*N *adequate and free Reprefentation of the People, fuited to the exifting ftate of fociety, is the life-fpring and mafter-principle of freedom in our Conftitution—*] Other writers might be adduced in proof of this point; but on this occafion I prefer Bifhop HURD's teftimony. Mr. PALEY and his admirers will more readily fubmit to epifcopal authority.

" In procefs of time, the leffer military tenants
" in *capite* multiplied exceedingly. And, as many
" of them were poor, and unequal to a perfonal
" attendance in the court of their lord, or in the
" common council of the kingdom (where of right
" and duty they were to pay their attendance) they
" were willing, and it was found convenient, to
" give them leave to appear in the way of *Reprefen-*
" *tation.* And this was the origin of what we now
" call the Knights of the Shires; who, in thofe
" times, were appointed to reprefent, not all the
" Freeholders of Counties, but the leffer tenants

" of

" of the Crown only. For thefe, not attending in
" perfon, would otherwife have had no place in the
" King's council.

" The rife of Citizens and Burgeffes, that is,
" Reprefentatives of the Cities and trading Towns,
" muft be accounted for fomewhat differently. Thefe
" had originally been in the jurifdiction, and made
" part of the demefnes of the King and his great
" Lords. The reafon of which appears from what
" I obferved of the genius of the feudal policy.
" For, little account being had of any but martial
" men, and trade being not only difhonourable, but
" almoft unknown in thofe ages ; the lower people,
" who lived together in towns, moft of them fmall
" and inconfiderable, were left in a ftate of fubjec-
" tion to the Crown, or fome other of the Barons,
" and expofed to their arbitrary impofitions and
" talliages.

" But this condition of Burghers, as it fprang
" from the military genius. of the nation, could only
" be fupported by it. When that declined there-
" fore, and inftead of a People of foldiers, the
" commercial fpirit prevailed, and filled our towns
" with rich traders and merchants, it was no longer
" reafonable, nor was it the intereft of the Crown,
" that thefe communities and bodies of men fhould
" be fo little regarded. On the contrary, *a large
" fhare of the public burdens being laid upon them,* and
" the frequent neceffities of the Crown, efpecially
" in foreign wars, or in the King's contentions with
" his Barons, *requiring him to have recourfe to their*
" *purfes,*

" purfes, it was naturally brought about that thofe, as
" well as the tenants in *capite, fhould in time be admitted*
" *to have a fhare in the public councils*."—*Moral and Po-*
litical Dialogues, by the Rev. Dr. HURD. *v.* 2. *p.* 156.
5*th Edit.*

" The Conftitution itfelf fuppofed the men of
" greateft confequence in the Common-wealth to
" have a feat in the national councils. Trade and
" agriculture had advanced vaft numbers into con-
" fequence, that before were of fmall account in
" the kingdom. The public confideration was in-
" creafed by their wealth, and the public neceffities
" relieved by it. Were thefe to remain for ever
" excluded from the King's councils? *or was not*
" *that council, which had Liberty for its object, to widen*
" *and expand itfelf in order to receive them?* It did,
" in fact, receive them with open arms; and, in fo
" doing, conducted itfelf on the very principles of
" the old feudal policy." *ib. p.* 166.

Note *B.* referred to from the note in p. 6.

The emiffary of a Tartar Mahometan Prince has pur-
chafed not lefs than EIGHT SEATS *among the Commons*
of Great Britain.—] Of this fact there can be no
doubt. Mr. PITT, when he brought forward his
firft Motion in favour of a Parliamentary Reform,
did not fcruple to affert it in the Houfe. " Another
" fet (he faid) of Boroughs and Towns, in the lofty
" poffeffion of Englifh Freedom, *claimed to them-*

" *felves*

" *felves the right of bringing their Votes to market.*
" They had no other property, no other ftake in
" the country, than the property and price which
" they procured for their votes. Such Boroughs
" were the moft dangerous of all others. So far
" from confulting the intereft of their country, in
" the choice which they made, they held out their
" Boroughs to the beft purchafer, and *in faɛt they*
" *belonged more to the* NABOB OF ARCOT *than they*
" *did to the People of Great Britain. They were Cities*
" *and Boroughs more within the jurifdiɛtion of the Car-*
" *natic than the limits of the Empire of Great Britain ;*
" *and it was a faɛt pretty well known and generally*
" *underftood, that the Nabob of Arcot had no lefs than*
" SEVEN *or* EIGHT MEMBERS *in that Houfe !* Such
" Boroughs then were fources of corruption ; they
" gave rife to an inundation of corrupt wealth and
" corrupt Members, who had no regard or connec-
" tion either for or with the People of this king-
" dom," &c. &c.—*Debrett's Parliamentary Regifter,*
v. 24. *p.* 124.

Mr. BURKE alfo harangues indignantly on this
abufe.—" Our wonderful Minifter, as you all know,
" formed a new plan, a plan *infigne recens alio in-*
" *diɛtum cre,* a plan for fupporting the freedom of our
" Conftitution by court intrigues, and for removing
" its corruptions by Indian delinquency. To carry
" that bold paradoxical defign into execution, fuffi-
" cient funds and apt inftruments became neceffary.
" You are perfectly fenfible that a Parliamentary
" Reform occupies his thoughts day and night, as

3   " an

" an effential member in this extraordinary project.
" In his anxious refearches upon this fubject, natura.
" inftinct, as well as found policy, would direct his
" eyes, and fettle his choice on PAUL BENFIELD.
" PAUL BENFIELD is the grand Parliamentary Re-
" former, the Reformer to whom the whole choir of
" Reformers bow, and to whom even the right ho-
" nourable gentleman [Mr. PITT] himfelf muft
" yield the palm: For what region in the empire,
" what City, what Borough, what County, what
" tribunal in this kingdom, is not full of his la-
" bours? others have been only fpeculators; he is
" the grand practical Reformer; and while the
" Chancellor of the Exchequer pledges in vain " *the*
" *man and the minifter,*" to increafe the provincial
" Members, Mr. Benfield has aufpicioufly and prac-
" tically begun it. Leaving far behind him even
" Lord *Camelford*'s generous defign of beftowing
" *Old Sarum* on the Bank of England, Mr. Ben-
" field has thrown in the Borough of CRICKLADE
" to reinforce the County Reprefentation. Not
" content with this, in order to ftation a fteady
" phalanx for all future Reforms, this public-fpirited
" ufurer, amid his charitable toils for the relief of
" India, did not forget the *poor rotten Conftitution* of
" his native country. For her, he did not difdain
" to ftoop to the trade of a wholefale upholfterer
" for this Houfe, to furnifh it, not with the faded
" tapeftry figures of antiquated merit, fuch as
" decorate, and may reproach fome other houfes,
" but with real, folid, living patterns of true

H 4   " modern

" modern virtue. *Paul Benfield made (reckoning*
" *himself) no fewer than* EIGHT *Members in the last*
" *Parliament.* What copious ſtreams of pure blood
" muſt he not have transfuſed into the veins of the
" preſent!"—*Works, v. 2. p. 511.*

Indeed, Mr. BURKE, commenting on the Nabob
of Arcott's private debts to Europeans being charged
on the revenues of the Carnatic, in the ſame Speech
heſitates not to impute that extraordinary tranſaction
to the Parliamentary intereſt of the Creditors in theſe
glowing words—" Let no man hereafter talk of the
" decaying energies of nature. All the acts and monu-
" ments in the records of peculation; the conſolidated
" corruption of ages; the patterns of exemplary
" plunder in the heroic times of Roman iniquity,
" never equalled the gigantic corruption of this
" ſingle act. Never did Nero, in all the inſolent
" prodigality of deſpotiſm, deal out to his prætorian
" guards a donation fit to be named with the largeſs
" ſhowered down by the bounty of our Chancellor
" of the Exchequer [Mr. PITT] *on the faithful band*
" *of his Indian Sepoys.*"

Both Mr. BURKE and Mr. PITT poſſeſſed peculiar
means of information reſpecting the number of
Members put into Parliament by the Nabob of
Arcot or his agent. Mr. BURKE's Brother (Mr. R.
BURKE) in an Election cauſe where Mr. PITT was
the junior Councel, took occaſion in addreſſing the
Jury to remark, " that the whole Weſt of England
" were anxious to ſee Mr. BENFIELD, and to partake
" of his liberality. That each Borough was de-
" ſirous

" firous of having him for their Reprefentative ; but
" his perfon could not be divided. That into
" Cricklade pouring the riches of the Eaft fhe foon
" fell a victim, and that Borough he fixed on himfelf
" to reprefent. That in the other Boroughs he had
" his fubftitutes, and NINE *of thofe fubftitutes, he then*
" *had in the Houfe of Commons*" !!—*Report of the*
Cricklade Cafe. p. 312.

Note C. referred to from p. 10.

" *The rotten part of our Conftitution, the fmall*
" *Boroughs*"—] The paffage in BURNET is as fol-
lows :—" Moft of the great Counties and the chief
" Cities chofe men that were zealous for the King and
" Government : but *the rotten part of our Conftitution,*
" *the fmall Boroughs,* were in many places wrought
" on to choofe bad men." *Hift. of his own Time.*
v. 2. *p.* 295. *fol.* 1734.

Note D. referred to from p. 22.

—*as the conftitutional principle of free and popular Elec-*
tion demands.] " If the King doth newly incor-
" porate an antient Borough (which fent Burgeffes
" to the Parliament) and granteth that certain
" felected Burgeffes fhall make Election of the Bur-
" geffes of Parliament, where all the Burgeffes
" elected

" elected before, this Charter taketh not the Elec-
" tion of the other Burgesses. And so, if a City, &c.
" hath power to make Ordinances, they cannot
" make an Ordinance that a lesse number shall elect
" Burgesses for the Parliament than made the Elec-
" tion before; *for free Elections of Members of the*
" *High Court of Parliament are pro bono publico,*
" and not to be compared to other cases of Election
" of Maiors, Bailiffs, &c. of Corporations."

COKE. 4 Inst. 48.

" In most parlements where I have served thirty
" years togither, whensoever any question came
" about the freedome of elections, I have observed
" *the inclination of the house of commons to favour*
" *the popular elections,* judging the more free and
' indifferent the election is, the more it is for the
" freedome and interest of the commons; wherof
" many precedents and judgments are in the jour-
" nals of that house: and before the statute 8 H. 6.
" which restraines elections to be by freeholders of
" 40 shillings per annum only, all the freeholders
" generally had their votes in thofe elections; and
" att this day in antient cittys and boroughs, for the
" most part the elections still remaine popular and
" free by all the inhabitants, except almes men and
" such like."—WHITELOCKE's *Notes uppon the King's
Writt for choosing Members of Parlement. v.* 1. *p.* 385.

.

Note

Note E. referred to from p. 23.

Your Law vaunts that Englishmen act in Legislation
" *either in person or by Representation upon their own*
" *free Elections.*"] This conftitutional principle is
to be found in the Parliamentary recognition of the
defcent of the Crown of England to JAMES, on the de-
mife of ELIZABETH. " As we cannot too often, or
" enough, fo can there be no means or ways fo fit,
" both to facrifice our unfeigned and hearty thanks to
" Almighty GOD, for bleffing us with a Sovereign
" adorned with the rareft gifts of mind and body, in
" fuch admirable peace and quietnefs, and upon the
" knees of our hearts to agnize our moft conftant
" faith, obedience, and loyalty to your Majefty and
" your royal progeny, as in this High Court of Par-
" liament, *where all the whole body •of the Realm,*
" *and every particular member thereof, either in Perfon*
" *or by Reprefentation* (UPON THEIR OWN FREE
" ELECTIONS) are by the Laws of this Realm
" deemed to be perfonally prefent." Stat. 1 Jac. 1. c. 1.

The introductory nonfenfe is amply compenfated
by this ftatutory declaration of the original and common right of Englifhmen. It is declaratory of the
Common Law; as will appear by the fucceeding
extract from Sir Tho. SMYTH's curious tract on the
" manner of Gouernement or policie of the Realme
" of Englande." This Gentleman, Secretary to
EDWARD and ELIZABETH, fays, " Euerie Englifh-
" man is entended to bee there [in Parliament]
" prefent;

" prefent, either in perfon or by procuration and
" attornies, of what preheminence, ftate, dignitie,
" or qualities foeuer he be, from the Prince (be he
" King or Queene) to the loweft perfon of Englande.
" And the confent of the Parliament is taken to be
" euerie mans confent." *De Republica Anglorum.*
1583. *p. 35.*

The fame doctrine is recognized by Mr. Juftice
BLACKSTONE.—" The Commons confift of all fuch
" men of property in the kingdom, as have not
" Seats in the Houfe of Lords : *every one of which*
" *has a voice in Parliament, either perfonally or by his*
" *Reprefentatives.* In a free State every man, who
" is fuppofed a free agent, ought to be in fome
" meafure his own governor ; and therefore *a branch*
" *at leaft of the legiflative power fhould refide in the*
" *whole body of the People.*"—*Commentaries on the
Laws of England. v.* 1. *p.* 158. 8vo.

Note F. referred to from p. 23.

—*outnumber the Conftituents of a Majority of your lower
Houfe of Legiflature.*] After the extracts in the Note
immediately preceding, the following ftatement cannot but fill every honeft mind with fcandal.—" Your
" Committee find that *two hundred and fifty-feven*
" Members, being a *Majority* of the Commons of
" England, are elected by *eleven thoufand and feventy-*
" *five voters* ; or in other words, by little more than
" the

" the *one hundred and feventieth part* of the People to
" be reprefented, even fuppofing them to be only *two*
" *millions.*"—*Report of the Committee of* THE FRIENDS
OF THE PEOPLE *on the Reprefentation of England
and Wales.* p. 5. 4to. *printed by order of the Society.*—
Scottifh Reprefentation lies in a ftate yet more de-
plorable.—" In two of the Counties, there are only
" *three* real Voters in each; in feven not more than
" *ten :* in all of them refpectively very few. The
" total number of real Voters in the whole Kingdom
" is *one thoufand three hundred and ninety.*"—*Report
of the Reprefentation of Scotland,* publifhed by the fame
Society, p. 8. 4to.

Note G. referred to from p. 23.

*Perpetuities and Reverfions of Seats among your Re-
prefentatives are advertized for fale by auction as publicly as feats at your Theatres.*] Within thefe few
years the perpetuity of nominating *two* Members for
Gatton, and a reverfion in fee to nominate *one* for
Afhburton, have been openly advertized and fold by
auction. Thefe anecdotes will form no uninterefting
part in the hiftory of Parliament, and fhould be
preferved.

" A MOST VALUABLE CONTINGENCY.

" Yefterday the fpirit and purity of the Englifh
" Conftitution was demonftrated in a very remark-
" able

" able manner.   The eftate of GATTON was fold by
" auction, and the value of the eftate was enhanced
" by a public declaration, that befide the rental, the
" manfions, the parks, the water, and fo forth, it
" poffeffed *moft valuable Contingencies*, which Mr.
" CHRISTIE faid, tho' they were of a nature too de-
" licate for him to mention, they were too palpable
" to be overlooked.

    " The contingency is, that *tho' there be three or*
" *four miferable hamlets on the eftate, lett at no more*
" *than forty fhillings a year rent, or thereabout, it fends*
" *two Members to Parliament.*   This contingency,
" which is valuable only on account of the cor-
" ruption of the day in which we live, has advanced
" this eftate beyond all credible eftimate ; and made
" it, for a certain clafs of men, one of the moft de-
" firable purchafes in England.   The rental is only
" fifteen hundred pounds a year, and therefore by
" the difproportioned fize of the manfions, parks,
" and offices, it can only be confidered as a country
" villa.

    " This villa was yefterday peremptorily fold at
" the hammer for fixty-two thoufand guineas !—and
" this fum was confidered as fo egregioufly beneath
" the value, that Mr. CHRISTIE held it for a very
" confiderable time in fufpence, before he would
" fuffer it to go at that fum.—

    " We muft bear teftimony to the able and mafterly
" manner in which Mr. CHRISTIE managed this
" fubject.   He hinted at the contingency with great
" nicety—He faid that in three years an occafion
                                      " .would

" would come when the aſtoniſhing importance of
" this eſtate would be felt—It was too conſpicuous to
" require comment—His eye traverſed the room for
" *Nabobs*. He hinted at inquiries and Impeach-
" ments—looked firſt to the Boroughmongers of
" one party, and then of another—He ſquinted at all
" the poſſible contingencies of political convul-
" ſion—and as an apology for dwelling on the in-
" adequate ſum of ſixty-two thouſand guineas, he
" begged the audience to reflect on a moment what
" muſt be the reflection thrown upon him three
" years hence, if he ſhould ſuffer it now to go at
" that ſum. " What ſhould I do (ſays he) three
" years hence, when, on the true value of this in-
" eſtimable purchaſe being known, it ſhould ſell for
" twenty or thirty thouſand pounds more than the
" preſent ſum ? What muſt I do in this caſe ? Why
" pulverize my hammer, and forſwear for eternity
" a profeſſion for which I ſhould be proved demon-
" ſtratively unfit !" It was at length knocked down
" to old Joſhua Sharp, who was ſaid to buy it for
" the Earl of Hertford. Edward Moore, Eſq; bid
" ſixty-one thouſand guineas. Mr. Sharpe offered
" another thouſand, and made the purchaſe.

" We forbear to comment on this ſubject. But
" ſurely, in the enſuing Seſſion this circumſtance
" will juſtify the arguments of Mr. F O X and Mr.
" P I T T, and convince Parliament, if reaſoning can
" convince them, of the neceſſity that there is for
" a Reform in the Repreſentation of the People."

GAZETTEER; *September* 8th, 1786.

" Devon-

" Devonſhire.

" To be peremptorily ſold,

By Mr. Chriſtie,

" At his Great Room in Pall Mall, on Wedneſday
" the 7th of February next, at one o'clock,

" The reverſion in fee, ſubject to two lives, a
" moiety of the Lordſhip, &c. &c. of ASHBURTON
" in the county of Devon, together with the Court
" Baron, Court Leet, and Perquiſites thereto be-
" longing, and the Rents payable by the Free or
" Burgage Tenants, in number one hundred and
" ſixty-three of the annual amount of twenty-two
" pounds and upward : the above comprehends

" *A moſt valuable Contingency*
" *of a deſirable nature, requiring no comment.*

" Printed particulars may be now had at the White
" Lyon Inn, Briſtol; York Houſe, Bath; White
" Hart, and Antelope, Saliſbury; the Rainbow
" Coffee-houſe, Cornhill; and in Pall Mall."

GAZETTEER; January 8th, 1787.

Note H. referred to from p. 31.

This Identity of Intereſt is to be attained by a partici-
pation of the People in their own Government—] " He
" that would know whether abſolute Monarchys or
" mix'd

" mix'd Governments do moſt foment or puniſh
" Venality and Corruption, ought to examine the
" principle and practice of both, and compare them
" one with the other. As to the Principle, the
" above mentioned Vices may be profitable to pri-
" vate men, but they can never be ſo to the
" Government, if it be popular or mix'd : No
" People was ever the better for that which renders
" them weak or baſe ; and *a* DULY CREATED *Ma-*
" *giſtracy, governing a Nation with their conſent, can*
" *have no intereſt diſtinct from that of the Publick,*
" or deſire to diminiſh the ſtrength of the People,
" which is their own, and by which they ſubſiſt.
" On the other ſide, the abſolute Monarch who
" governs for himſelf and chiefly ſeeks his own
" preſervation, looks upon the ſtrength and bravery
" of his Subjects as the root of his greateſt danger,
" and frequently deſires to render them weak, baſe,
" corrupt, and unfaithful to each other, that they
" may neither dare to attempt the breaking of the
" yoke he lays upon them, nor truſt one another in
" any generous deſign for the recovery of their
" Liberty. So that the ſame corruption which pre-
" ſerves ſuch a Prince, if it were introduced by a
" People, would weaken, if not utterly deſtroy
" them." *Diſcourſes concerning Government ; by* AL-
GERNON SIDNEY. *ch.* 2. *Sect.* 19.

Note

Note I. referred to from p. 33.

Making the total number of Patrons only, &c.] I subjoin the paffage at large.

" The Patronage of which your Petitioners com-
" plain, is of two kinds; *That* which arifes from
" the unequal diftribution of the Elective Franchize,
" and the popular rights of voting by which cer-
" tain places return Members to ferve in Parlia-
" ments; and *that* which arifes from the expence
" attending contefted Elections, and the confequent
" degree of power acquired by wealth.

" By thefe two means, a weight of Parliamentary
" Influence has been obtained by certain indivi-
" duals, forbidden by the fpirit of the Laws, and
" in its confequences moft dangerous to the Liber-
" ties of the People of Great Britain.

" The operation of the *firft* fpecies of Patronage
" is direct, and fubject to pofitive proof. EIGHTY-
" FOUR *individuals do by their own immediate autho-*
" *rity fend* ONE HUNDRED AND FIFTY-SEVEN *of*
" *your Honourable Members to Parliament. And this*
" *your Petitioners are ready, if the fact be difputed, to*
" *prove, and to name the Members and the Patrons.*

" The *fecond* fpecies of Patronage cannot be
" fhown with equal accuracy, though it is felt with
" equal force.

" Your Petitioners are convinced, that in addi-
" tion to the *one hundred and fifty-feven Honourable*
" *Members above mentioned, one hundred and fifty*
" *more, making in the whole* THREE HUNDRED AND
                                          " SEVEN,

" SEVEN, *are returned to your Honourable House, not*
" *by the collective voice of those whom they appear to*
" *represent, but by the recommendation of* SEVENTY
" *powerful individuals, added to the* EIGHTY-FOUR
" *before-mentioned, and making the total number of*
" *Patrons altogether* ONLY ONE HUNDRED *and* FIFTY
" FOUR, *who return a decided majority of your Ho-*
" *nourable House.*"—*Authentic Copy of a Petition pray-*
ing for a Reform in Parliament; presented to the House
of Commons on 6th May, 1793; published by the So-
ciety, THE FRIENDS OF THE PEOPLE, *associated for the*
purpose of obtaining a Parliamentary Reform. p. 11. 4to.

Note K. referred to from p. 34.

The Lower House, I fear, carries in its prominent
features too many infallible tendencies toward an oligar-
chical and standing SENATE.] Mr. BURKE many
years ago made the same complaint.—" An ad-
" dressing House of Commons, and a petitioning
" Nation; an House of Commons *full of confidence,*
" when the Nation is plunged in despair; in the
" utmost harmony with Ministers, whom the People
" regard with the utmost abhorrence; who vote
" Thanks, when the Public Opinion calls upon
" them for Impeachments; who are *eager to grant,*
" *when the general voice demands account;* who, in all
" disputes between the People and Administration,
" presume *against* the People; who punish their

I 2   " dif-

" diforders, but refufe even to enquire into the pro-
" vocations to them; this is an unnatural, a mon-
" ftrous ftate of things in this Conftitution. Such
" an affembly may be a great, wife, aweful SENATE ;
" *but it is not to any popular purpofe an Houfe of*
" *Commons.* This change from an immediate ftate
" of procuration and delegation to a courfe of act-
" ing as from original power, is the way in which
" all the popular magiftracies in the world have
" been perverted from their purpofes." *Works. v.*
1. *p.* 464. Again : " The conftant habit of au-
" thority, and the unfrequency of Elections, have
" tended very much to draw the Houfe of Com-
" mons toward the character of *a ftanding* SENATE."
ib. p. 465.—And the *Yorkfhire Committee* adopted the
fame diftinction.—" The balance of our Conftitu-
" tion had been wifely placed by our forefathers in
" the hands of the Counties and principal Cities and
" Towns; but by the caprice and partiality of our
" Kings, from Henry 6th down to Charles 2d, it
" was gradually withdrawn from them, and by *the*
" *addition of Two Hundred Parliamentary Burgeffes, was*
" *wholly vefted in the inferior Boroughs.* From that
" latter period, the mifchiefs of this irregular exer-
" cife of royal authority have been farther increafed
" by the filent operation of time. Many unre-
" prefented Towns have rifen into population,
" wealth, and confequence, in the kingdom; many
" Boroughs have funk into indigence, or have even
" totally difappeared, without a trace of their exift-
" ence left behind them, except the privilege of
" nominal

" nominal Reprefentation. *In thefe decayed Bo-*
" *roughs, the Crown and a few great Families noto-*
" *rioufly nominate Reprefentatives, who form a clear*
" *Majority of the Houfe of Commons.* In that Ma-
" jority a liberal Minifter will ever find a ready fup-
" port, however ruinous the meafures of his admi-
" niftration may be to the Liberty and the general
" intereft of his country. The Members who re-
" prefent the great maffes of landed and commercial
" property, fhall plead in vain for their Confti-
" tuents. *In the fcale of Parliamentary computation,*
" *an inconfiderable village will balance a County; and a*
" *fhort lift of hamlets, where hardly a veftige of popu-*
" *lation is to be found, will decide againft the general*
" *fenfe and wifhes of the Public.* A Parliament elected
" *in any reafonable proportion, would duly reprefent the*
" *fenfe, and act for the intereft of the whole community;*
" *but from a* SENATE *thus unequally arranged, no penal*
" *Laws, no external regulations can exclude corruption;*
" *becaufe in fituations of no control, partial advantage*
" *will ftill outweigh the public good.* In royal inno-
" vation this grofs abufe in the Reprefentation of
" the People chiefly originates. From Parliamen-
" tary Authority a proper counterpoize, to thefe
" dependent Boroughs, muft be reftored to the
" Counties and principal Cities, &c. before that
" Affembly can become once more a firm and in-
" corruptible guardian of the public weal."—*Ad-*
drefs from the Committee of Affociation of the County of
York to the Electors of Great Britain: WYVILL'S *Po-*
litical Papers, v. 1. *p.* 310.

Note

Note L. referred to from p. 38.

The magnitude of this Debt, and the concomitant extent of Taxation—] To aggravate the alarming consequences of our immense Debt, if I had the inclination, would be needless, after the warning of the Commissioners appointed by the Legislature to examine the Public Accounts.—" It is expedient
" (they reported to the House of Commons) that
" the true state of the National Debt should be
" disclosed to the Public; every subject ought to
" know it, for every subject is interested in it. This
" Debt is swelled to a magnitude that requires the
" united efforts of the ablest heads and purest hearts,
" to suggest the proper and effectual means of re-
" duction. The Nation calls for the aid of all its
" members to co-operate with Government, and to
" combine in carrying into execution such measures
" as shall be adopted, for the attainment of so in-
" dispensible an end: this aid the subject is bound
" to give to the State, by every other obligation,
" as well as by the duty he owes to his country; and,
" with such general aid, the difficulties, great as
" they appear, will, we trust, be found not insur-
" mountable. A plan must be formed for the re-
" duction of this debt, and that without delay; now,
" in the favourable moments of Peace. The evil
" does not admit of procrastination, *palliatives, or*
" *expedients:* it presses on and must be met with force
" and firmness. The right of the public creditor
" to his Debt, must be preserved inviolate: his se-
" curity

" curity refts upon the folid foundation, never to be
" fhaken, of Parliamentary national faith." &c.
&c. See their *eleventh Report.*

On the extent of our Taxation, I fhall extract
from the works of Mr. ARTHUR YOUNG fome curious calculations. I have no other wifh than that
they may ftrike conviction as forcibly on others as
they do on myfelf.

" I have fo often, in this memoir, mentioned the
" weight of our Taxes, and there are fo many per-
" fons who confider fuch things flightly, and with-
" out applying calculation to them, that I am ap-
" prehenfive left any reader fhould imagine, that I
" deal more in general declamation on the fubject,
" than proceed on the authority of well founded
" facts. To obviate this idea, and give the beft
" proof I can poffibly quote of the juftice of my
" complaints, I will produce that inftance with
" which I am unqueftionably well acquainted, name-
" ly, my own property. I have near a nominal
" 300l. a year here ; the following detail of Taxes
" will fhow, that it is *but nominal.* I muft premife,
" that I reckon the Tythe, Rates, and Windows of
" two or three tenants, the fame in the account as
" if paid by myfelf; for they are in fact as much
" paid by me, as the fums fo affeffed on my own
" farm ; of this the proof is fufficiently clear, to
" thofe who have tythe free, or extra-parochial
" farms to let ; the rent is exactly proportioned to
" fuch circumftances. Thefe burthens fall on a
" given portion of landed property; it matters no-

I 4 " thing

" thing by whofe hand they are paid ; the proprietor
" will be fure to feel that all iffues from his pocket.

		£.	s.	d.	£.	s.	d.
" Tythe—my own *,	- £.	31	0	0			
" A Tenant,	- -	10	0	0			
" Ditto,	- - -	10	0	0			
					51	0	0
" Poor Rates,	- -	33	0,	0			
		10	0	0			
		7	0	0			
		3	0	0			
					53	0	0
" Land Tax,	- - - -				39	12	0
" Road duty and turnpike,	- -				5	6	0
" Affeffed taxes,	- -	18	17	6			
		7	7	0			
		1	0	0			
		0	8	0			
					27	12	6
" Manor of Bradfield Combuft, Caftle " Guard rent,	- - - -				0	4	5
" Lands in Bradfield Combuft, Caftle " Guard rent,	- - - -				0	2	8
" Feudal quit rent,	- - -				2	2	7
" Confumption of malt in " the family, 6 qrs. at " 14s. 6d. a qr. tax,	- - -				4	7	0

Carry forward 183 7 2

" * Mr. Burke's expreffion made me fmile, " revenues
" which *taken from no perfon*, are fet apart for virtue !"

" Pay

	£.	s.	d.
Brought forward	183	7	2

" Pay annually to my own
" labourers 33l. in lieu
" of beer, which, in the
" fame ratio, is for the
" tax,   -   -   -   11   19   3
" 36 acres of barley, an-
" nually; produce 4 qrs.
" 144 qrs. pay in malt
" tax 2l. 18s. an acre;
" and if 3 qrs. of this crop
" (deducting 4 bufhels
" for feed, and 4 more
" for hogs, poultry, &c.)
" are brewed into 7¼ bar-
" rels of ale, at 5s. 10d.
" a barrel duty, it is
" 2l. 5s. 2¼d. per acre,
" together 5l. 3s. 2½d.
" per acre; while the to-
" tal value of the produce
" of the eaftern counties
" of the kingdom, does
" not exceed, at 20s. the
" fum of 4l. A produce
" taxed like this, at 125
" per cent. of the value,
" muft be leffened in the
" confumption and price
" greatly: I fhall fuppofe,

" to

$£.$ $s.$ $d.$

Brought forward $£.$ 11 19 3   183 7 2

" to avoid all exaggera-
" tion, that this deduction
" in price, is only 4s. a
" qr. on the 3 qrs. per
" acre fold, this forms a
" tax of   -   -   - 21 12 0

                    —————— 33 11 3

" The fale of wool of my
" own flock, amounts to
" 30l. a year; the depref-
" fion of the price, by
" reafon of the cruel mo-
" nopoly given by our
" laws, to the manufac-
" turers, has been clearly
" proved, in various paf-
" fages of this work, to
" amount on carding
" wool to 10 per cent. of
" the value,   -   -

                    —————— 3 0 0
                    ——————
                    219 18 5

" N. B. On combing wool it is cent. per cent.

" Of the numerous duties on confumption, in
" the form of Cuftoms, Excifes, Stamps, and in-
" cidents, I have calculated my payments, but do
" not include them in this account, as they are
                                    " more

" more connected with income, in general, than
" with the fpecified receipt, from a given portion
" of land; I will, however, remark, in order to
" inftigate others to make fimilar calculations, which
" are really curious exhibitions of Taxation, that
" for my confumption of wine, tea, fugar, candles,
" foap, infurance againft fire, ftamps, falt, and
" coals, I pay the fum of 26l. 4s. 5d. exclufive of
" the further articles of leather, glafs, currants,
" raifins, fpices, drugs, deals, iron, hemp, flax,
" rum, brandy, printed linen, paper, &c. &c.
" Thefe would probably raife the fum to 40l.

" But recurring folely to the 219l. 18s. 5d. the
" amount of the taxes paid by my eftate, let me
" next explain what it pays me as proprietor.

		£.	s.	d.
" Grofs rental,	- - - -	295	3	0
" Deductions—Land tax, £. 39 12 0				
" Quit rent, - - 2 2 7				
" Caftle Guards, - - 0 7 1				
" Repairs, on the average				
" of 7 years, - - 23 8 9				
		65	10	5
" Nett receipt, - - - -		229	12	7

" Hence it appears, that out of a portion of
" land which yields the proprietor 229l. 12s. 7d.
" the public burthens take 219l. 18s. 5d. ! ! !

" To what region of defpotifm, monarchical or
" republican, are we to go, to meet with any thing
" equal

" equal to this? And does it not hence appear,
" that I have not complained of the cruelty, ine-
" quality, and injustice of Taxation in this kingdom,
" without sufficient ground; but have justly attri-
" buted to their baneful influence, the ruin of all
" the little estates in the kingdom?"—*Annals of
Agriculture. v.* 15. *p.* 186.

———————

Note M. referred to from p. 38.

—*Parliament after Parliament, the ready responsive*
Aye *to Ministerial requisitions to take the People's money?*] A respected Member of the Legislature
ascribes the facility of Parliament to grant money
to the same cause—" Our not possessing a House of
" Commons, connected with and dependent on the
" People; unconnected with and independent of
" the Crown." In the same inedited tract, enforcing
the necessity of a Parliamentary Reform, this Gentleman continues pointedly but truly, let " the Na-
" tion take a general review of their History since
" the Revolution, and of their present situation,
" On that view, let them determine for themselves,
" whether, in the nature of things, it be possible
" that, in so short a period, the blood of this
" country should have been wasted in so many fo-
" reign wars; such treasures should have been la-
" vished away, sometimes in the support of inter-
" ests, in which we had no essential concern, and
. " sometimes in the destruction of interests, which
" were

" were our own, or ought to have been equally
" dear to us; that fuch a national income as ours
" fhould have been exhaufted, fuch a Debt in-
" curred, and fuch enormous burthens as actually
" exift, impofed upon the People of this Ifland,
" and of which the direct Taxes of the State are
" only a part;—if the Houfe of Commons had been
" what it ought and profeffes to be, a true Repre-
" fentative of and Fellow Sufferer with the Peo-
" ple, an effective controul over the Minifters of
" the Executive Power, the faithful Stewards of the
" public Purfe, and not, what it is, a power iden-
" tified with that of the Crown. The virtue, fpirit,
" and effence of a Houfe of Commons confifts in
" its being the exprefs image of the feelings of the
" Nation. What fympathy, what community of
" feeling is there between the hand that pays the
" tax, and the hand that receives it;—between him
" whofe intereft it is that the amount fhould be
" moderate, and him, whofe intereft it is that the
" amount fhould be exorbitant?" *p.* 8.

Note N. referred to from p. 43.

*Perjury, of which Election-Oaths are the main
fource, and Cuftom-houfe and Excife-Oaths the tributary
ftreams,* &c.] The following paffage contains a
practical example of the lamentable effects arifing
from fuch debafement of the fanctity of an oath.—

" An

" An extraordinary affair happened once at Lowef-
" toff, when his friend Mr. Clarke was with him
" upon a vifit; which, he fays, they never forgot.
" They went together on board one of the fmall
" trading fhips belonging to that town, and there
" obferved two feamen jointly lifting up a veffel out
" of the hold: when another who ftood by afked
" one of them, who was looking down it, why he
" did not turn his face away? upon which he turned
" his face away, but continued to affift in lifting as
" before. The meaning of which they underftood
" to be this; that he would be obliged to fwear, he
" *faw* nothing taken out of the hold, not that he
" *took* nothing out of it. This, fays Mr. Whifton,
" is a feaman's falvo for fuch errant perjury; and
" *this is the confequence of our multiplying oaths on*
" *every trifling occafion.*"—See *Hiftorical Memoirs of*
the Life of Dr. Samuel CLARKE, *p.* 5. Or the *General*
Biographical Dictionary, under the Article WHISTON.

Note O. referred to from p. 45.

The interference of the Lords of Parliament—to be an
high infringement upon the Liberties and Privileges of
the Commons.] Extract of the Addrefs and Refolutions of the Society of the FRIENDS OF THE PEOPLE.
Freemafon's Tavern, 9th April, 1794.—" Surely at a
" moment when the excellence of the Conftitution
" is

" is fo vigoroufly maintained, that to propofe
" amendment is looked upon as feditious, its
" advocates will at leaft be as ftrenuous in de-
" fence of what they acknowlege to be its efta-
" blifhed principles, as they are active in founding
" the alarm againft whatever they choofe to call an
" innovation. If that fpirit of difcontent really pre-
" vails, which high authority fo very confidently
" announces, all good men will be anxious to re-
" move every plaufible ground of complaint; and,
" above all, the Houfe of Commons will be cautious
" how they tolerate a violation of the Conftitution,
" which they have themfelves fpecifically defined
" and reprobated; and to which, by their Votes,
" they have called the public attention.

‘ From the year 1701 to the year 1794, the
‘ Houfe of Commons have, at the commencement
‘ of every Seffion, uniformly paffed the following
‘ Refolution: That it is a high infringement upon
‘ the Liberties and privileges of the Commons of
‘ Great Britain, for any Lord of Parliament, or any
‘ Lord Lieutenant of any County, to concern them-
‘ felves in the Elections of Members to ferve for the
‘ Commons in Parliament.’

" In their Petition of laft year, the Society com-
" plained of the frequent violation of this excellent
" Refolution, and brought the queftion before the
" Houfe of Commons in thefe words:" ‘ Your
‘ Petitioners inform your Honourable Houfe, and
‘ are ready to prove it at your bar, that they have
‘ the moft reafonable grounds to fufpect that no

‘ lefs

' lefs than ONE HUNDRED AND FIFTY of your
' Honourable Members owe their Elections intirely
' to the interference of Peers; and your Petitioners
' are prepared to fhow by legal evidence that forty
' Peers, in defiance of your refolutions, have poffeffed
' themfelves of fo many Burgage tenures, and ob-
' tained fuch an abfolute and uncontroled command
' in very many fmall Boroughs in the kingdom, as
' to be enabled, by their own pofitive authority,
' to return EIGHTY-ONE of your Honourable Mem-
' bers.'

" The Society again repeat this in the face of the
" country; and they earneftly intreat every friend
" to the Liberties of England, to take into con-
" fideration the confequences of fo alarming a
" practice.

" As far as depends on them, the Society, with-
" out hefitation, lead the way to bring the queftion
" to iffue, and therefore,

" Refolve unanimoufly :—

" I. That the People have a right to the pure,
" genuine, and uncorrupted energy of the Englifh
" Conftitution, faithfully adminiftered according to
" its own acknowleged principles.

" II. That the Commons of Great Britain, in
" Parliament affembled, have, fince the reign of
" King William III. uniformly, folemnly, and an-
" nually determined one of thofe principles to be
" violated, whenever a Peer interferes in an Elec-
" tion.

" III. That

" III. That Peers at this day do interfere in
" Elections, not only by the exercise of the influ-
" ence naturally arising from high rank and exten-
" five possessions, but *by embarking large portions of*
" *their wealth in the purchase of Borough-Property,*
" *notoriously for the purpose of sending Members into the*
" *House of Commons.*

" IV. That above *one fourth* of the present House
" of Commons owe their Seats to the known influ-
" ence and interference of Peers.

" V. That this interference has a tendency to
" destroy those advantages, which are to be derived
" from preserving the separate branches of the Legi-
" stature distinct and independent of each other, and
" to make the House of Commons an engine of the
" Crown and Nobility, instead of what it ought to
" be—A CHECK UPON THE KING AND THE LORDS.

" VI. That the great number of Gentlemen well
" known to be concerned in Borough-Speculations,
" who, *by the advice of the Minister, have been created*
" *Peers,* demands the most serious consideration of
" every friend to the Constitution of Great Britain.

" VII. That the People of this Country ought
" not to be taxed but by the consent of Repre-
" sentatives chosen by the free Suffrages of the
" Commons of Great Britain; and that a daring
" insult is offered to the Constitution of these
" Realms whenever a Peer attempts to usurp the
" Nomination of a Member to serve in Parliament.

" In name, and by order of the society,

" WM. BRETON, Chairman."

Note P. referred to from p. 52.

You have graduated a moral barometer to ascertain the various degrees of guilt contracted by the various stages of inebriety.] Here is Mr. Paley's attempt to determine quality by quantity. "If the privation "of reason be only partial, the guilt will be of a "mixt nature. For so much of his self-govern- "ment, as the drunkard retains, he is as respon- "sible then, as at any other time. He is entitled "to no abatement, beyond the strict proportion, "in which his moral faculties are impaired. Now "I call the guilt of the crime, if a sober man had "committed it, the *whole* guilt. A person in the "condition we describe, incurs part of this, at the "instant of perpetration, and by bringing himself "into this condition, he incurred *such a fraction of* "*the remaining part, as the danger of this consequence* "*was of an integral certainty !* For the sake of illus- "tration, we are at liberty to suppose, that a man "loses half his moral faculties by drunkenness ; this "leaving him but half his responsibility, he incurs, "when he commits the action, *half of the whole* "*guilt.* We will also suppose that it was known "before hand, that it was an even chance, or half "a certainty, that this crime would follow his "getting drunk. This makes him chargeable with "*half of the remainder* ; so that altogether, he is "responsible for *three-fourths of the guilt,* which a "sober man would have incurred by the same "action.

"I do

" I do not mean that any real cafe can be reduced
" to numbers; or the calculation made with arith-
" metical precifion; but thefe are the principles,
" and this the rule, by which our general admeafure-
" ment of the guilt of fuch offences, fhould be
" regulated." *p.* 319.

Note Q. referred to from p. 54.

—*Great and unconftitutional Influence of the Crown.*]
" Petition agreed to at the Meeting of the County
" of York, held the 30th day of December, 1779,
" which having been afterward circulated through
" the County, was figned by near *nine thoufand*
" Freeholders, and prefented by Sir George Savile
" to the Houfe of Commons on the 8th day of
" February, 1780.

" To the Honourable the Commons of Great
        ' " Britain in Parliament affembled.

" The Petition of the Gentlemen, Clergy, and
        " Freeholders of the County of York,

        " Sheweth,
        " That this Nation hath been engaged for feveral
" years in a moft expenfive and unfortunate War;
" that many of our valuable Colonies have actually
" declared themfelves independent, have formed a
" ftrict confederacy with France and Spain, the
" dangerous and inveterate enemies of Great Britain;

" that

" that the confequence of thefe combined mis-
" fortunes hath been a large addition to the national
" Debt; a heavy accumulation of Taxes; a rapid
" decline of the trade, manufactures, and land-rents
" of the kingdom.

" Alarmed at the diminished refources and grow-
" ing burthens of this country, and convinced that
" rigid frugality is now indifpenfibly neceffary in
" every department of the State, your Petitioners
" obferve with grief, that, notwithftanding the
" calamitous and impoverished condition of the
" Nation, *much public money has been improvi-*
" *dently fquandered, and that many individuals enjoy*
" *finecure places, efficient places with exhorbitant*
" *emoluments, and penfions unmerited by public fer-*
" *vice,* to a large and ftill encreafing amount;
" whence the Crown has acquired a GREAT
" AND UNCONSTITUTIONAL INFLUENCE, *which, if*
" *not checked, may foon prove fatal to the Liberties*
" *of this country.*

" Your Petitioners, conceiving that the true end
" of every legitimate Government is not the emolu-
" ment of any individual, but the welfare of the
" community; and confidering that, by the Con-
" ftitution of this realm, the national purfe is en-
" trufted in a peculiar manner to the cuftody of this
" Honourable Houfe, beg leave farther to reprefent,
" that until effectual meafures be taken to redrefs
" the oppreffive grievances herein ftated, the grant
" of any additional fum of public money, beyond
" the produce of the prefent Taxes, will be injuri-

" ous

" ous to the rights and property of the People, and
" derogatory from the honour and dignity of Par-
" liament.

" Your petitioners, therefore, appealing to the
" juſtice of this Honourable Houſe, do moſt
" earneſtly requeſt that, before any new burthens
" are laid upon this country, effectual meaſures
" may be taken by this Houſe, to inquire into and
" correct the groſs abuſes in the expenditure of
" public money; to reduce all exhorbitant emolu-
" ments; to reſcind and aboliſh all ſinecure places
" and unmerited penſions; and to appropriate the
" produce to the neceſſities of the State in ſuch
" manner as to the wiſdom of Parliament ſhall ſeem
" meet.

" And your petitioners ſhall ever pray, &c."

WYVILL's *Political Papers*, *v.* 1. *p.* 7.

The following Counties preſented Petitions nearly
in the ſame words:

Middleſex, Dorſet, Cheſter, Devon,
Hants, Norfolk, Hertford, Berks,
Suſſex, Bucks, Huntingdon, Nottingham,
Surrey, Kent, Cumberland, Northumberland,
Bedford, Suffolk, Eſſex, Hereford,
Glouceſter, Cambridge, Someiſet, Derby,
Wilts.

Alſo the Cities of London, Weſtminſter, York,
Briſtol, and the Towns of Cambridge, Nottingham,
Newcaſtle, Reading, and Bridgewater.—The County
of Northampton agreed to inſtruct their Members
on the points of the Petition.

K 3   " Die

" Die Veneris, Aprilis 14mo. 1780.

" Moved,

" That the Bill, intitled a Bill for the exclufion
" of Contractors from the lower Houfe of Parlia-
" ment, be read a fecond time and committed.

" After fome debate, the queftion being put,
" there appeared

  " For the commitment — 41
  " Againft it — — 60
          ——

    " Majority — 19

" It was then moved to reject the Bill.

" The queftion was put thereupon, and refolved
" in the affirmative.

" Diffentient,

" I. Becaufe the Commons, defirous of re-efta-
" blifhing the reputation and authority of Parlia-
" ment, and of giving fatisfaction to the People,
" at a time when the moft cordial and unfufpicious
" confidence between the reprefentative and confti-
" tuent bodies is effentially neceffary, have come to
" a Refolution, ' That it is neceffary to declare,
" that the Influence of the Crown has increafed, is
" increafing, and ought to be diminifhed.'

" This Refolution we conceive to be undeniably
" true, and highly feafonable. Their commence-
" ment of the diminution (which they have folemnly
" engaged to make) by their Bill here rejected, is
" no lefs judicious. In the midft of a War, in
" which nothing (among all its unhappy circum-
" ftances) is more remarkable than the prodigality
          " with

" with which it is carried on, it appears peculiarly
" neceffary to remove from Parliament the fufpicion
" that the rafh adoption, the obftinate continuance,
" and the corrupt fupply of military arrangements,
" are connected with the fupport of a court majority
" in Parliament.

" II. Becaufe *the People, oppreffed with actual im-*
" *pofitions, and terrified with the certain profpect of*
" *farther and heavier burthens, have a right to be*
" *affured, that none fhould have a power of laying thofe*
" *burthens, who have an intereft in increafing them.*
" *Neither is it fit that they who are the principal fub-*
" *jects of complaint, fhould fit as the controllers of their*
" *own conduct.* Contracts can never be fairly made,
" when the Parliamentary fervice of the Con-
" tractor is a neceffary, underftood part of the
" agreement, and muft be reckoned into the price.
" But the moft unexceptionable Contract being a
" matter of great advantage to the Contractor, it
" becomes a means of Influence even when it is not
" a principle of abufe. It is the greateft of all the
" bribes a Minifter has to beftow ; and one day's
" jobb may be worth the purchafe of the fee of moft
" of the Places and Penfions that are held in that
" Houfe.

" III. Becaufe no reafons have been affigned for
" the rejection of this Bill, but fuch as appear to
" us frivolous or dangerous. It was argued as
" neceffary to abate the phrenzy of virtue, which
" began to fhow itfelf in the Houfe of Commons.
" This new fpecies of phrenzy we look upon to be

" rather

" rather a character of foundneſs, than a ſymptom
" of infanity; and we fairly declare, that, as we
" frequently come into contact with the other
" Houſe, we heartily wiſh that that diſtemper may
" become contagious. Another reaſon aſſigned
" againſt this Bill, *that it is not poſſible for vaſt*
" *pecuniary emoluments to have any Influence on Mem-*
" *bers of Parliament, appears to originate from ſo per-*
" *feēt a puerility of underſtanding, or ſuch a contempt*
" *of that of the Houſe and the Nation, that it is men-*
" *tioned as a matter to be animadverted upon, not*
" *anſwered.* Of the ſame nature is the argument
" drawn from the ſuppoſed improbability of abuſes
" in contraēts, becauſe the Law has left in the hands
" of the Miniſters the means of proſecuting at law
" the ſupporters of their power, and the accomplices
" of their own fraud and malverſation. Theſe argu-
" ments will give little ſatisfaction to thoſe who look
" at the Houſe of Lords as a barrier againſt ſome
" poſſibly ſudden and miſtaken warmth of the Houſe
" of Commons, that might be injurious to the juſt
" Prerogatives of the Crown, or the Rights of the
" People; but we will not bear the groſs abuſe of
" this conſtitutional power ; or that this Houſe
" ſhould ſet itſelf as an obſtruction to the moſt
" honourable, manly, and virtuous Reſolution, ever
" come to by an Houſe of Commons ; a reſolution
" made in direct conformity to the Petitions of their
" Conſtituents. *We proteſt, therefore, againſt our*
" *ſtanding in the way of even the firſt ſteps taken toward*
" *promoting*

" *promoting the independence, integrity, and virtue of a*
" *House of Parliament.*

" De Ferrars,	J. St. Afaph,
" Rockingham,	Beaulieu,
" Abergavenny,	Ofborne,
" Fortefcue,	Cholmondeley,
" Courtenay,	Manchefter,
" Wycombe,	Coventry,
" Ponfonby,	St. John,
" Percy,	Fitz-William,
" Ferrers,	Abingdon,
" Pembroke, and	Portland,
" Montgomery,	Devonfhire,
" Scarborough,	Harcourt,
" Richmond,	Jerfey.

" For the firft and third reafons, adopting how-
" ever very heartily in the prefent ftate of Parlia-
" mentary Reprefentation the found principles con-
" tained in the fecond, which yet I conceive inap-
" plicable to this Bill.

" Radnor."

Note R. referred to from p. 62.

—*fcandalous practices acquired in the Court of the*
defpot, where he fpent his early life.] CLARENDON relates and laments this bias. On the introduction of a
French cuftom at the Coronation of Charles he ob-
ferves—" They liked it the worfe, becaufe they
" difcerned

" difcern..d that it iffued from a fountain, from
" *whence many bitter waters were like to flow,* the
" *cuftoms of the Court of France, whereof the King*
" *and the Duke had too much the image in their heads,*
" and than which there could not be a copy more
" univerfally ingrateful and odious to the Englifh
" Nation." *Life of Clarendon, by himfelf,* v. 1.
p. 367. 8vo. 1760—And again : " Not only the
" Duke, but the King himfelf, had a marvellous
" prejudice to the Nation [the Englifh] in that part
" of good manners : And it was eafily agreed that
" *the model of France,* was in thofe, *and other cafes,*
" *much more preferable,* and which was afterward ob-
" ferved in too many." *ib.* v. 2. *p.* 76.—Add to
thefe—" *After the Reftoration, England adopted the*
" *modes of France, her worft modes.* There were
" fome, too many, who, unworthy of their own
" happinefs and Liberty, came to admire her Go-
" vernment and misfortune ; and laboured with the
" fpirit of Parricides, though without their punifh-
" ment, to bring ours to the model of that." *The*
works of Tacitus, with political Difcourfes, by T.
GORDON, *v.* 4. *p.* 210. *4th edit.*

" The French greatnefs never, during his whole
" reign, infpired Charles with any apprehenfions ;
" and CLIFFORD, it is faid, one of his moft fa-
" voured Minifters, went fo far as to affirm that *it*
" *were better for the King to be Viceroy under a great*
" *and generous Monarch, than a flave to five hundred*
" *of his own infolent fubjects !*" HUME ; *Hift. of Eng-*
land. v. 8. *p.* 203. 8vo.

Note S. referred to from p. 64.

Not to multiply authorities—] Left I fhould too much encumber the text with quotations, I forbore to infert any more than the opinions of CLARENDON, BOLINGBROKE, and BURKE. Here, to confront the *" many wife and virtuous politicians who* (as *Mr.* PALEY *" tells us) deem a confiderable portion of Influence to be a " neceffary part of the Britifh Conftituticn"*—p. 491. but whofe names he gives not, I muft add the concordant authorities of Lord LYTTLETON, Judge BLACKSTONE, Sir William JONES, and Bifhop WATSON.—" I fhall only add to what I have faid, that, " unlefs fomething be done by this Parliament, to " give new vigour to our Liberties, ftop the torrent " of Corruption, and revive the principles and the " fpirit of our fathers, we have lefs *to hope than to " apprehend from thofe to come.* The time, I doubt, is " not far off, when by the increafe of Influence, " there may be fuch difficulties upon country Gentle- " men to oppofe the Court in Elections, and fuch " a defpondency, fuch a difpiritednefs on the minds " of all, except the favourites of power, that no " ftruggle could be expected, no oppofition at all, " to the nomination of the Crown. A kind of *congé " d'elire* might be fent down into the country, and " directed to our trufty and well-beloved officers of " the Cuftoms, Excife, and Army, in all the Towns " and Boroughs of England, Scotland, Wales, and

" the

" the Duchy of Cornwall. Suitable returns would
" be made : but, Sir, *this would not be a Parliament.*"
LYTTLETON ; *Works by Ayfcough, v.* 1. *p.* 107.

" With regard to power, we may find perhaps that
" the hands of Government are at leaft fufficiently
" ftrengthened ; and that an Englifh monarch is now
" in no danger of being overborne by either the
" Nobility or the People. The inftruments of
" Power are not perhaps fo open and avowed as
" they formerly were, and therefore are the lefs
" liable to jealous and invidious reflections ; but they
" are not the weaker upon that account. In fhort,
" our national Debt and Taxes (befides the incon-
" veniences before-mentioned) have alfo in their
" natural confequences thrown fuch a weight of
" power into the executive fcale of Government, as
" we cannot think was intended by our patriot an-
" ceftors ; who glorioufly ftruggled for the abolition
" of the then formidable parts of the Prerogative ;
" and by an unaccountable want of forefight efta-
" blifhed this fyftem in their ftead. The entire
" collection and management of fo vaft a Revenue
" being placed in the hands of the Crown, have
" given rife to fuch a multitude of new officers,
" created by and removeable at the royal pleafure,
" that they have extended the Influence of Govern-
" ment to every corner of the nation. Witnefs the
" Commiffioners, and the multitude of the de-
" pendents on the Cuftoms, in every port of the
" kingdom ; the Commiffioners of Excife, and their
" numerous

" numerous fubalterns, in every inland diftrict; the
" Poftmafters and their fervants, planted in every
" town, and upon every public road; the Com-
" miffioners of the Stamps, and their diftributors
" which are full as fcattered and full as numerous;
" the officers of the falt duty, which, though a fpe-
" cies of Excife, and conducted in the fame manner,
" are yet made a diftinct corps from the ordinary
" managers of that revenue; the furveyors of houfes
" and windows; the receivers of the land tax; the
" managers of Lotteries, and the Commiffioners of
" hackney coaches; all which are either mediately
" or immediately appointed by the Crown, and re-
" moveable at pleafure, without any reafon affigned:
" thefe, it requires but little penetration to fee, muft
" give that power, on which they depend for fub-
" fiftance, an Influence moft amazingly extenfive.
" To this may be added the frequent opportunities
" of conferring particular obligations, *by preference in*
" *Loans, Subfcriptions, Tickets, remittances, and other*
" *money-tranfactions, which will greatly increafe this*
" *Influence; and that over thofe perfons whofe attach-*
" *ment, on account of their wealth, is frequently the moft*
" *defirable.* All this is the natural, though perhaps
" the unforefeen, confequence of erecting our Funds
" of credit, and to fupport them eftablifhing our pre-
" fent perpetual Taxes: the whole of which is entirely
" new fince the Reftoration in 1660; and by far the
" greateft part fince the Revolution in 1688. And ·
" the fame may be faid with regard to the officers
" in our numerous Army, and the places which the

" Army

" Army has created.   All which put together, give
" the executive power fo perfuafive an energy with
" refpect to the perfons themfelves, and fo pre-
" vailing an intereft with their friends and families,
" as will amply make amends for the lofs of ex-
" ternal prerogative."   BLACKSTONE ; *Comment.*
b. 1. *ch.* 8.

    " Return a conciliating Parliament, and reftore
" the loft balance of your Conftitution.   I faid the
" *loft* balance, and I faid it with boldnefs ; becaufe
" it is a propofition of the cleareft evidence, a truth
" of the firft water, that the due temperature of
" powers in our mixed fyftem, which MONTESQUIEU,
" who breathed the fpirit of an Englifhman, and
" BLACKSTONE, who was the pride of England, fo
" lavifhly applauded, fubfifts no more.
    " The fubject, on which I am entering, is vaft,
" but I will reftrain myfelf within proper bounds,
" and be fatisfied with reminding you, that the exe-
" cutive Magiftrate (of whom it behoves us to
" fpeak refpectfully, yet freely) has of late acquired
" two enormous branches, not of juft prerogative,
" but of unconftitutional power : *Influence*, by re-
" ceiving and difpenfing at pleafure all the gold, and
" force, by commanding and fubjecting to his nod
" all the fteel, of the Nation, thus holding in his
" mighty grafp, as the Thunderer of the ancients is
" reprefented on Olympus, the two finews of war ;
" by one of which the coequal parts of the Legifla-
" ture may continually be fapped, and by the other

2   " may

" may at any time be ftormed. I have heard undue
" Prerogative compared to a giant, who beftrides
" our narrow ifland, and may at his difcretion
" fufpend his maffy club over our heads, or reduce
" us to powder with its weight; while Influence re-
" fembles a fairy, who plays around us invifibly, or
" affumes any fhape that fuits her purpofe, and
" often drops *gold or patents* in proper places, as a
" reward or incentive for fuch as merit the approba-
" tion of the little wanton divinity. Attempts to
" bring back the Conftitution to its genuine tem-
" perament are fo far from being feditious, or even
" derogatory from the refpect due to the Crown,
" that they would, if fuccefsful, highly augment the
" fplendour of it; unlefs it be more glorious to
" rule, like the princes of the continent, over flaves,
" than to be the chief in a Nation of Freemen; an
" opinion, which no man, who deferves either dig-
" nity or freedom, can entertain." *Speech by Sir W.*
JONES, *in* 1780. *p.* 53.

 " For my own part, and I verily believe I am far
" from being fingular in my notions, I take this op-
" portunity of publicly declaring to your Grace,
" what I have a thoufand times before declared to
" my friends in private, that I never entertained the
" moft diftant defire, of feeing either the Demo-
" cratical, or the Ariftocratical fcale of the Confti-
" tution, outweigh the Monarchical; not one jot of
" the legal Prerogative did I ever wifh to fee abo-
" lifhed; not one tittle of the King's Influence in
         " the

" the State to be deftroyed, except fo far as it was
" extended over the deliberations of the Hereditary
" Counfellors of the Crown, or the Parliamentary
" Reprefentatives of the People. I own I have
" wifhed, and I own (with a heart as loyal as the
" loyaleft) that I fhall continue to wifh, that an In-
" fluence of this kind may be diminifhed; becaufe
" I firmly believe that its diminution will, eventually
" tend to the confervation of the genuine Confti-
" tution of our country; to the honour of his Ma-
" jefty's Government; to the ftability of the
" Hanover fucceffion; and to the promotion of the
" public good. Had the Influence here fpoken of
" been lefs predominant of late years; had the
" meafures of the Cabinet been canvaffed by the
" wifdom, and tempered by the moderation of men
" exercifing their free powers of deliberation for the
" common weal, the brighteft jewel of his Ma-
" jefty's crown had not now been tarnifhed; the
" ftrongeft limb of the Britifh Empire had not now
" been rudely fevered from its parent ftock. I
" make not this remark with a view of criminating
" any fet of Minifters, (for the beft may be miftaken
" in their judgments, and errors which are paft
" fhould be forgotten, buried in the zeal of all
" parties to rectify the mifchiefs they have occa-
" fioned) but fimply to fhow, by a recent example,
" that the Influence of the Crown when exerted by
" the Cabinet, over the Public Counfellors of the
" King, is a circumftance fo far from being to be
" wifhed by his true friends, that it is as dangerous
" to

" to the real interefts and honour of the Crown
" itfelf, as it is odious to the People, and deftructive
" of public Liberty ; it may contribute to keep a
" prime Minifter in his place contrary to the fenfe
" of the wifeft and beft part of the community ; it
" may contribute to keep the King himfelf un-
" acquainted with his People's wifhes, but it cannot
" do the King or the State any fervice. *To maintain*
" *the contrary is to fatyrize his Majefty's Government,*
" *it is to infinuate that his views and interefts are*
" *fo disjoined from thofe of his People, that they cannot be*
" *effectuated by the uninfluenced concurrence of honeft*
" *men.* It is far beneath the character of a great and
" upright Monarch, to be fufpected of a defire to
" carry any plans of Government into execution in
" oppofition to the fentiments of a free and en-
" lightened Parliament ; and the Minifter who
" fhould be bafe enough to advife him to adopt
" fuch an arbitrary fyftem of Government, or fhould
" fupply the corrupted means of carrying it on,
" would deferve the execration of every man of in-
" tegrity, and would, probably, fooner or later, meet
" with the deferved deteftation of the Prince him-
" felf. It is of fuch men as thefe—there is no
" impropriety, I hope, in borrowing truth from tra-
" gedy, fince Chryfoftom is faid to have flept with
" even an Ariftophanes under his pillow ; it is of
" fuch men as thefe the poet fpeaks,

> " It is the curfe of Kings to be attended
> " By flaves that take their humour for a warrant ;
> " And who, to be endeared to a King,
> " Make no confcience to deftroy his honour.

L   " In

' In a word, if there be any one meafure more
" likely than another to preferve pure and un-
" blemifhed the honour of the Crown; to fecure its
" moft valuable rights; to procure for it warm,
" bold, determined friends, who in the hour of dan-
" ger would fupport it at the hazard of their lives
" againft foreign or domeftic infult; I verily believe
" it to be, the eftablifhing, as much as poffible, *the*
" *independency of the feveral Members of both Houfes of*
" *Parliament.*" WATSON's *Sermons and Tracts.*
p. 407. 1788.

Note T. referred to from p. 67.

*Sometimes was mortified by fullen expoftulation, not to
fay rude remonftrance.*] To take one inftance.

" My Lords and Gentlemen,

" I have a full affurance of the good affections of
" my People; which I fhall endeavour to preferve,
" by a conftant care of their juft Rights and Li-
" berties; by maintaining the eftablifhed Religion;
" by feeing the courfe of Juftice kept fteady and
" equal; by countenancing virtue, and difcouraging
" vice; and by declining no difficulties nor dangers,
" where their welfare and profperity may be con-
" cerned. Thefe are my refolutions; and I am
" perfuaded that you are come together with pur-
" pofes, on your part, fuitable to thefe of mine.
" Since, then, our aims are only for the general
" good, let us act with confidence in one another;
                                        " which

" which will not fail by Gᴏᴅ's blessing to make
" me a happy King, and you a happy, flourishing
" People."

" This excellent speech was so far from removing
" (as it was hoped) the ill impressions, which the
" dissatisfaction the King had expressed upon the
" proceedings of the Commons, when he parted
" with them last, had left in their minds, that it
" served rather to increase them. The Commons,
" notwithstanding their disbanding the forces, would
" not suffer the least intimation of their want of con-
" fidence in the King; and grew angry at their
" being thought to have given any occasion to such
" a suspicion: Instead, therefore, of an address of
" thanks, they presented a sort of remonstrance,
" setting forth; " That, being highly sensible that
" there was nothing more necessary for the peace
" and prosperity of the kingdom, for the quieting
" People's minds, and disappointing his enemies
" designs, than a mutual and entire confidence be-
" tween him and his Parliament; they did esteem
" it their greatest misfortune, that, after having so
" amply provided for his and the Government's se-
" curity, both by sea and land, any jealousy or mis-
" trust had been raised of their duty and affection to
" him and his People: And beg leave to represent
" to him, that it would greatly conduce to the con-
" tinuing and establishing an entire confidence be-
" tween him and them, that he would show marks
" of his high displeasure toward all, that should pre-
" sume to misrepresent their proceedings to him;

L 2   " and

" and they, on their part, being duly fenfible of
" his conftant concern to maintain their civil and
" religious Rights, in defence whereof he had fo
" often expofed his perfon, would do all they could
" to prevent and difcourage all falfe rumours and
" reports, reflecting on his Majefty's Government,
" whereby to create any mifunderftanding between
" him and his fubjects." *Hift. of England; continua-*
tion of RAPIN *by* TINDAL, *v.* 4. *p.* 256. *fol.*

Note U. referred to from p. 69.

—-*from the Statute of Talliage to the Speeches of*
CAMDEN *againft American Taxation*—]

" My fearches have more and more convinced
" me, that the Britifh Parliament have no right to
" tax the Americans. I fhall not, therefore, con-
" fider the declaratory Bill now lying on your table;
" for to what purpofe, but lofs of time, to confider
" the particulars of a Bill the very exiftence of
" which is illegal, abfolutely illegal, contrary to the
" fundamental laws of Nature, contrary to the
" fundamental laws of this Conftitution? A Con-
" ftitution grounded on the eternal and immutable
" laws of Nature; a Conftitution whofe foundation
" and centre is Liberty, which fends Liberty to
" every fubject that is, or may happen to be within
" any part of its ample circumference. Nor, my
" Lords, is the doctrine new; 'tis as old as the
" Con-

" Conſtitution; it grew up with it; indeed it is its
" ſupport; *Taxation and Repreſentation are inſe-*
" *parably united;* GOD hath joined them, no Bri-
" tiſh Parliament can ſeparate them; to endeavour
" to do it is to ſtab our very vitals. Nor is this
" the firſt time this doctrine has been mentioned;
" ſeventy years ago, my Lords, a pamphlet was
" publiſhed recommending the levying a Parlia-
" mentary Tax on one of the Colonies; this pam-
" phlet was anſwered by two others, then much
" read; theſe totally deny the power of taxing the
" Colonies; and why? becauſe the Colonies had no
" Repreſentatives in Parliament to give conſent; no
" anſwer, public or private, was given to theſe
" pamphlets, no cenſure paſſed upon them; men
" were not ſtartled at the doctrine, as either new or
" illegal, or derogatory to the rights of Parliament.
" I do not mention theſe pamphlets by way of au-
" thority, but to vindicate myſelf from the imputa-
" tion of having firſt broached this doctrine.

" My poſition is this—I repeat it—I will main-
" tain it to my laſt hour,—*Taxation and Repreſenta-*
" *tion are inſeparable;* this poſition is founded on the
" laws of Nature; for whatever is a man's own is
" abſolutely his own; no man has a right to take it
" from him without his conſent, either expreſſed by
" himſelf or Repreſentative; whoever attempts to
" do it attempts an injury; *whoever does it, commits*
" *a robbery;* he throws down and deſtroys the diſ-
" tinction between Liberty and ſlavery. *Taxation*
" *and Repreſentation are coeval with and eſſential to*

2   " *this*

" *this Conſtitution.* I wiſh the maxim of MACHIA-
" VEL was followed, that of examining a Conſtitu-
" tion at certain periods, according to its firſt prin-
" ciples; this would *correct abuſes, and ſupply de-*
" *fects.* I wiſh the times would bear it, and that
" men's minds were cool enough to enter upon ſuch
" a taſk, and *that the repreſentative authority of this*
" *kingdom was more equally ſettled."* Lord CAMDEN'S
Speech againſt the Bill declaratory of the Sovereignty of
Great Britain over the Colonies, in 1766.

Note W. referred to from p. 76.

In turning over the leaves of your production we per-
petually recal the ſentiments of former writers, fre-
quently copied literally, and always without acknow-
legement.] Take theſe as a ſpecimen.

LOCKE had ſaid:

" We may, I think from the
" make of *an Oyſter or Cockle,*
" reaſonably conclude that it
" has not ſo many, nor ſo quick
" ſenſes, as a Man, or ſeveral
" other Animals; nor if it
" had, would it in that ſtate,
" and incapacity of transfer-
" ring itſelf from one place to
" another, be bettered by them.
" I cannot but think, there is
" ſome ſmall dull perception,
" whereby they are diſtin-
" guiſhed

And Mr. PALEY ſays:

" When we are in perfect
" health and ſpirits, we feel in
" ourſelves a happineſs inde-
" pendent of any particular
" outward gratification what-
" ever, and of which we can
" give no account. This is an
" enjoyment which the Deity
" has annexed to life; and
" probably conſtitutes, in a
" great meaſure, the happineſs
" of infants and brutes, eſpe-
" cially of the lower and ſe-
" dentary

" guished from perfect insensi-
" bility. And that this may
" be so, we have plain in-
" stances, even in mankind it-
" self. Take one in whom
" decrepid old age has blotted
" out the memory of his
" past knowlege, and clearly
" wiped out the Ideas his mind
" was formerly stored with ;
" &c. How far such an one
" (notwithstanding all that is
" boasted of Innate Princi-
" ples) is in his knowledge and
" intellectual faculties above
" the condition of *a Cockle or*
" *an Oyster,* I leave to be con-
" sidered." *An Essay concerning Human Understanding, b.
2. ch. 9. v. 1. p.* 109. *of 8th
edit. 8vo.* 1721.

" dentary orders of animals,
" as *oysters, periwinkles,* and the
" like ; for which I have some-
" times been at a loss to find
" amusement." *b.* 1. *ch.* 6. *p.*
33, *of 1st edit.*

Locke had said :

" That men should keep
" their compacts, is certainly
" a great and undeniable rule
" in Morality : But yet, if a
" Christian, who has the view
" of Happiness and Misery in
" another life, be asked why
" a Man must keep his word,
" he will give this as a reason :
" Because GOD, who has the
" power of eternal Life and
" Death, requires it of us.
" But if an Hobbist be asked
" why,

And Mr. PALEY says :

" Why am I obliged to keep
" my word ? Because it is
" right, says one.—Because it
" is agreeable to the Fitness
" of Things, says another.—
" Because it is conformable to
" Reason and Nature, says a
" third.—Because it is con-
" formable to Truth, says a
" fourth.—Because it promotes
" the Public Good, says a
" fifth.—Because it is required
" by the Will of GOD, con-
" cludes,

" why, he will anfwer, becaufe
" the Public requires it, and
" the Leviathan will punifh
" you if you do not. And if
" one of the old Heathen Phi-
" lofophers had been afked,
" he would have anfwered,
" becaufe it was difhoneft, be-
" low the dignity of a Man,
" and oppofite to Virtue, the
" higheft perfection of human
" Nature, to do otherwife."
ib. b. 1. *ch.* 3. *p.* 32 *of fame vol.*
of fame edit.

" cludes a fixth," *b.* 2. *ch.* 1.
p. 47. *of fame edit.*

BLACKSTONE of Marriage.

" The Civil Law required
" the confent of the Parent or
" Tutor at all ages; unlefs
" the children were emanci-
" pated, or out of the Parents
" power.——Thefe provifions
" are adopted and imitated by
" the French and Hollanders,
" with this difference: that
" in France the Sons cannot
" marry without confent of
" Parents till thirty years of
" age, nor the Daughters till
" twenty-five; and in Holland,
" the Sons are at their own
" difpofal at twenty-five, and
" the Daughters at twenty.
" Thus hath ftood, and thus
" at prefent ftands, the Law
" in other neighbouring coun-
" tries.

Mr. PALEY of Marriage.

" A late regulation in the
" law of Marriages in this
" Country, has made the con-
" fent of the Father, if he be
" living, of the Mother, if fhe
" furvive the Father, or of
" Guardians, if both Parents
" be dead, neceffary to the
" Marriage of a perfon under
" twenty-one years of age. By
" the Roman Law, the confent
" *et avi et patris* was required
" fo long as they lived. In
" France the confent of Pa-
" rents is neceffary to the Mar-
" riage of Sons, until they at-
" tain to thirty years of age;
" of Daughters, until twenty-
" five. In Holland for Sons,
" till twenty-five; for Daugh-
" ters

" tries. And it has lately been
" thought proper to introduce
" somewhat of the same policy
" into our Laws, by Statute
" '26 Geo. 2nd. c. 33. where-
" by it is enacted, that all
" Marriages celebrated by Li-
" cence, where either of the
" parties is under twenty-one,
" without the consent of the
" Father, or, if he be not liv-
" ing, of the Mother, or
" Guardians, shall be abso-
" lutely void." *Commentaries
on the Laws of England, b.* 1.
ch. 15. *v.* 1. *p.* 437. *of* 5*th edit.*
8*vo.* 1773.

" ters till twenty." *b.* 3. *part*
3. *ch.* 8. *p.* 281, *of* 1*st edit.*

Note X. referred to from p. 88.

Like MANDEVILLE *you would qualify your system
by setting bounds to the practice.*] Where I write, I
have not the *Fable of the Bees* at hand. But we
may safely rely on the representation of WARBUR-
TON. Of this preacher of a new Morality (for
MANDEVILLE called his book " a system of most
" exalted Morals") that learned Prelate indignantly
observes " though his general position be, that *pri-*
" *vate vices are public benefits*, yet, in his proof of
" it, he all along explains it by *vice only in a certain
" measure, and to a certain degree.*" *Divine Legation
of Moses demonstrated. b.* 1. *s.* 6.

M   Note

Note Y. referred to from p. 91.

" *The Army muſt have its pay, and the Public Cre-*
" *ditors their intereſt.*"]

" They [the Houſe of Commons] poſſeſs a pre-
" tended power of with-holding Supplies. But the
" ſituation of ſociety has in truth wreſted it from
" them. The Supplies they muſt vote, for the
" Army muſt have its pay, and the Public Credi-
" tors their intereſt. A power that cannot be exer-
" ciſed without provoking mutiny, and proclaiming
" bankruptcy, the blindeſt bigot cannot deny to be
" purely *nominal.*" *Vindiciæ Gallicæ; by James*
MACKINTOSH, *Eſq. p.* 335. *2nd. edit.*

So JUNIUS.
" As to the refuſal of Supplies, we might puniſh
" ourſelves indeed, but it would be no way com-
" pulſory upon the King. With reſpect to his
" Civil Liſt, he is already independent, or might
" be ſo, if he had common ſenſe, or common re-
" ſolution; and as for refuſing to vote the Army or
" Navy, I hope we ſhall never be mad enough to
" try an experiment every way ſo hazardous." *Laſt*
Letter.

Note Z. referred to from p. 98.

The Sicilians inſulted with the ſolemn grimace of a
Parliament:] As I learn from a modern traveller.
" The

" The foundation of the Feudal Syftem was firft
" laid here by the count Rugeiro, about the middle
" of the eleventh century, immediately after he had
" driven the Saracens out of the Ifland. He di-
" vided Sicily into three parts; the firft, by con-
" fent of his army, was given to the church; the
" fecond he beftowed upon his officers, and the
" third he referved for himfelf.

" Of thefe three branches, or as they call them
" *Braccios*, (arms) he compofed his *Parliament, the*
" *form of which remains exactly the fame to this day.*
" The *Braccio Militare* is compofed of all the ba-
" rons of the kingdom to the number of two hun-
" dred and fifty-one, who are ftill obliged to mili-
" tary fervice : their chief is the prince Butero, who
" is hereditary prefident of the Parliament; for in
" conformity to the genius of the feudal govern-
" ment fome of the great offices are ftill hereditary.
" The three archbifhops, all the bifhops, abbeys,
" priors, and dignified clergy, amounting to near
" feventy, form the *Braccio Ecclefiaftico*. The arch-
" bifhop of Palermo is their chief. The Braccio
" Demaniale is formed by Election, like our Houfe
" of Commons : there are forty-three royal cities,
" ftiled *Demaniale*, that have a right to elect mem-
" bers. *Every Houfeholder had a vote in this Election.*
" Their chief is the Member for Palermo ; who is
" likewife prætor (or mayor of the city). He is
" an officer of the higheft rank, and his power is
" very extenfive, inferior only to that of the Vice-
" roy ; in whofe abfence the greateft part of the

2 " authority

" authority devolves upon him. He has a company
" of grenadiers for his body guards; and receives
" the title of excellency.

" The prætor, together with fix fenators, who
" are ftiled patricians, have the entire management
" of the civil government of the city. He is ap-
" pointed every year by the king, or by the vice-
" roy, which is the fame thing; for I don't find
" that the People any longer exercife even the form
" of giving their votes. So that the very fhadow
" of Liberty has now difappeared as well as the
" fubftance. You may judge of the fituation of
" Liberty in a kingdom, where all courts, civil and
" criminal, are appointed by regal authority, and
" where all offices are conferred only by the will of
" the Sovereign, and depend entirely upon his ca-
" price." *A Tour through Sicily and Malta; by P.*
BRYDONE, *F. R. S. v.* 2. *p.* 226. 1773.

THE END.

www.ingramcontent.com/pod-product-compliance
Lightning Source LLC
Chambersburg PA
CBHW021111020726
47500CB00003B/706